PUFFIN BOOKS

A HARAPPAN ADVENTURE

Sunila Gupte is the author of three children's books, *From Pumpkins to Pickles*, *Quest for the Quetzal Feather* and *The Adventure of the Missing Dancing Girl*. Her short stories for young readers have frequently featured in *The Hindu*, *Deccan Herald* and other newspapers. Currently, she lives in Bangalore.

Other Books in the *Girls of India* Series

GIRLS OF INDIA

A HARAPPAN ADVENTURE

SUNILA GUPTE

ILLUSTRATED BY HEMANT KUMAR

PUFFIN BOOKS

PUFFIN BOOKS

Published by the Penguin Group

Penguin Books India Pvt. Ltd, 11 Community Centre, Panchsheel Park, New Delhi 110 017, India

Penguin Group (USA) Inc., 375 Hudson Street, New York, New York 10014, USA

Penguin Group (Canada), 90 Eglinton Avenue East, Suite 700, Toronto, Ontario, M4P 2Y3, Canada (a division of Pearson Penguin Canada Inc.)

Penguin Books Ltd, 80 Strand, London WC2R 0RL, England

Penguin Ireland, 25 St Stephen's Green, Dublin 2, Ireland (a division of Penguin Books Ltd)

Penguin Group (Australia), 707 Collins Street, Melbourne, Victoria 3008, Australia (a division of Pearson Australia Group Pty Ltd)

Penguin Group (NZ), 67 Apollo Drive, Rosedale, Auckland 0632, New Zealand (a division of Pearson New Zealand Ltd)

Penguin Books (South Africa) (Pty) Ltd, Block D, Rosebank Office Park, 181 Jan Smuts Avenue, Parktown North, Johannesburg 2193, South Africa

Penguin Books Ltd, Registered Offices: 80 Strand, London WC2R 0RL, England

First published in Puffin by Penguin Books India 2013

Text copyright © Sunila Gupte 2013
Illustration copyright © Hemant Kumar 2013

All rights reserved

10 9 8 7 6 5 4 3 2 1

ISBN 9780143332091

Typeset in Mercury Text G4 by R. Ajith Kumar, New Delhi
Printed at Thomson Press India Ltd, New Delhi

ALWAYS LEARNING   **PEARSON**

For Kanchan, Arjun, Diya, Roshni,
Tahira and Ahaan

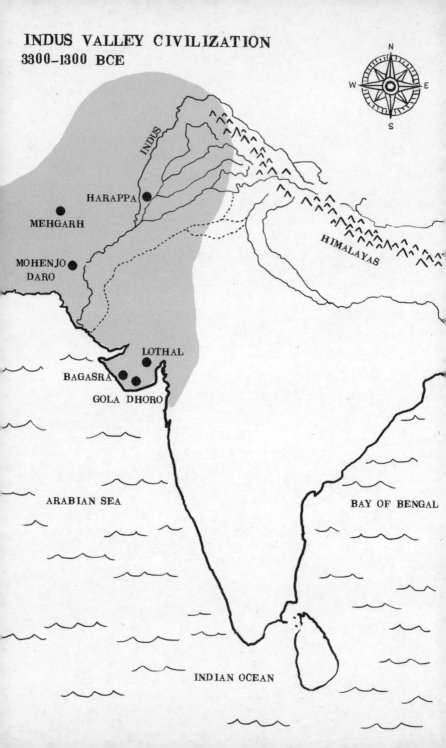

CONTENTS

1

CAPTURED!

It was the year 2570 ... yes, 2,570 years before Christ was born. Just above the great Taklamakan Desert in Central Asia, known in the local dialect as the 'go-in-and-you-will-not-come-out' desert, walked a lone figure, stooping with fatigue. He breathed a sigh of relief at having crossed this dreaded place safely.

Suddenly he was caught and held in a painfully tight grip.

'Don't move! Do as you are told, old man, or you will be very sorry,' ordered a harsh, guttural voice. It belonged to a rough-looking bandit.

'Indeeya! Shindu! Meluhha, Meluhha!' muttered the man, Zhao Gao, groaning.

A Chinese with an air of quiet dignity about him, he was dressed in the robes of a monk, with his long hair braided into a pigtail. His hands were pulled unmercifully behind him, and with a rough push he was made to roll further on the dry, stony ground. He felt a searing pain as his hands were quickly tied. His bundles were opened and the contents scattered around in disgust . . . nothing of value there!

Where were his disciples, Li Jinsong and Wu Shaozu? he wondered. Why could they not see he needed help? In a blur, he remembered that they had gone ahead of him, running to check if there was a caravanserai close by. Night was approaching, the sun would soon set and the terrain was unfriendly and hostile.

They had walked too slowly. He was now tired.

It had been a long, long journey of two years from his land in the plains of the Yellow River in southern China. They had taken a longer route, as they had heard that there was a chance of coming across brigands and bandits on the Silk Route. They had thought they would find oases and shelter on the other route. They did manage to find various traders, who were good to them, as soon as they saw that the monk had not come to trade, and did not bring Chinese silk or medicinal herbs or precious gems. Taking the circuitous way also meant that different rivers would make the journey to Meluhha less arduous. Crossing mountain ranges like the Pamir and Karakoram would have tired them more.

Again he wondered about his disciples. As his mind cleared, he realized he could no longer see them. Maybe they had been attacked as well! After all these weeks, bandits had finally got them. These thoughts raced through his dazed mind even as he was pulled and pushed and thrown to the ground.

Suddenly he heard a new voice, raised in anger and fear . . . but not at him.

'You fool! Can you not see that he is a holy person, a

monk? He is wounded! We leave religious people alone! Untie him! Be gentle! Beg his pardon. Where is your older brother? He should know better, letting you work alone!'

In front of Zhao Gao now stood a bandit with a long, light brown beard, wearing a rough tunic and a thick gold chain. He placed his right hand on his heart, bowed low and said in a rough but respectful tone, 'I beg your pardon! Forgive me, forgive him. He is stupid, he does not know. He has never seen a monk.' He then turned to his left.

'Help him to sit properly. Get water, honey, dates!' he shouted to another small, unkempt man who had just come up, panting.

Hastily the two men helped untie the monk, who even now did not have any anger on his face. Blood trickled from his nose and lips.

'Look at him. Could you not tell he is a MONK? Treat him with respect,' the bandit with the long brown beard shouted again.

The other two immediately complied and Zhao Gao was helped up. His eyes shone with a brilliant light, now that he had recovered a little. His voice was soft. Like most travellers he spoke a mixture of languages, which the bandits could understand.

'Forgive them, they know not what they do. My sons, I carry no jewels, no things to be bartered. I go only with the little I need for my long, arduous journey to Meluhha. Of worldly goods I have none. I only bring my prayer beads, my prayer flags, my little travelling altar, my jade disc and tubes, and my incense sticks, which I put in front of my ancestors and deities . . . these I need for prayer.' He paused, then asked, 'And have you also attacked my two good boys, the companions sent to look after me? I can no longer see them.'

The robbers looked at their leader.

'If you mean the two men who were ahead of you, yes, we have them,' the younger one confessed reluctantly.

'Release them too!' ordered the bandit lord—for he was the lord, as his gold chain proclaimed to all.

The minions ran to obey his commands.

The hard-eyed bandit who had tied Zhao Gao up reflected on the frail-looking monk. Not once had he shouted or resisted in any way. Nor had he tried to kick or bite, unlike the other two 'wild animals', he thought, rubbing his knee where he had got badly kicked. No, this man was different—serene, with only his long, narrow eyes blazing. However, this very calmness was frightening.

The monk stood rubbing his wrists, pulling his disarrayed, rough robe closely around himself. He looked at the sore, bloodied red welts made by the scratchy rope on his wrists, yet uttered not a word. His dark eyes were luminous with knowledge and he seemed to look beyond the human gaze.

The bandit lord, on bended knees, clutched the monk's robe. He could feel the power emanating from the holy man. His composure, his stillness spoke of strength and purpose.

'Forgive me, Your Holiness,' the bandit lord pleaded again. 'We will clean your wounds. We will let you and your disciples go as well. We never harm monks, God's chosen ones. We will return your belongings.

'We know not where you are bound but we will help— food, water sources, travel, mules to carry you, anything—

only don't bring forth the wrath of the gods and our ancestors on us and our families.'

'Indeeya . . . Shendu . . . Meluhha,' murmured Zhao Gao. 'We have to get there. For my gods have sent me on a holy mission.'

Sometime later, two puzzled, shamefaced men brought back the horrified and angry disciples, Li Jinsong and Wu Shaozu. Both the young monks were thin, wiry and strong, with slanting eyes and braided hair.

'We were a bit violent with them. Seeing they came from the land of the Yellow River, we thought they would have silk, ceramics, jade, iron, salt or other riches to be traded,' explained the younger bandit meekly.

The bandit lord turned to the two young monks, bowed and said, 'Please pardon us. Now go and look after your master, for he may be suffering from shock and injuries.'

The disciples walked to the monk, looking worried. How greatly harmed was he? They touched him gently and checked him for bruises and pain.

Jinsong nodded his head. 'Our master has suffered, and we must look after him,' he told the bandit chief. 'We have medicinal herbs and dried oranges, which will help him.'

Impatiently, the bandit lord said to his minions, 'You idiots! Get some walnuts, or the fresh figs and grapes from Fergana valley. Light a fire! Set up a yurt! That's our collapsible shelter of sticks, for the nights are cold,' he explained to the monks.

The younger bandits were dumbstruck. How their master had changed! He was considerate, respectful and helpful. They had never seen the chief so attentive before. Certainly this monk must be must be a venerable, important person!

Zhao Gao was also given a hot, reviving *shurpa* made of chickpeas, meat and vegetables, with sesame bread called *non*. The stony-faced younger bandits noted, Ah, their best food!

The monk assured the bandit that he had been forgiven and formally introduced the young disciples.

'Only recently have I learnt from fellow travellers from Mesopotamia and Magan that here, Indeeya is called Meluhha,' he said. 'We call it Shendu in China, after the river Sindhu.'

The bandit chief pressed one hand to his heart again and spoke, 'So to Meluhha you go . . . your journey is for the gods, you say. I will make all the arrangements; I know these unforgiving mountains—every frozen pass, every small path, rivers which freeze or flood . . . I have friends who will help you once you cross over. I myself will guide you first.

'Please carry our food for your journey. We have *suzma*, or what you call cottage cheese, dried *suzma* balls, and *kurtob*. In these leather-skin bags there is some *katyk* for you to drink. It is a strengthening sour milk drink. We will also give you some precious turquoise and lapis lazuli from the valley of the Pamir mountains to barter, and a little gold to help you onwards.'

Soon the bandit lord was planning their route with great thoroughness. Finally the monk and his disciples, Jinsong and Shaozu, got more help than they had imagined or hoped for, because the bandit lord had a relay of people to go ahead and inform about their requirements. He decided that for the monk it would be better to go by sea, from the port town of Sutkagen Dor on the Makaran coast to the town of Lothal, which was on the coast of the Gulf of Kambhat.

'Holy Sir, you can rest while we are travelling by boat, and reach refreshed and ready for your journey to the temple,' the bandit lord told the monk.

So it was decided and the three monks set off. The unusually high waves carried their boat to the dock in Lothal where ships anchored during high tide. Meluhha, Indeeya, finally!

2

MAROONED

Avani sat alone on the small raft, her heart thudding wildly against her ribs, and threw the rope over a boulder. Then she got off, taking the rope, carefully walking over the slimy boulders. She found a stable rock and tied the rope to it. Ah ... that jutting-out tree, standing all by itself, would be a good landmark to find the raft later.

She felt calmer now, though she was still scared. After all, she had come alone to 'Bhoot Byet' or Ghost Island, the name she and her friends had given the little bit of land they could see when they were out on the river. There were all kinds of rumours surrounding it: 'It's a bad place. There are bad spirits there. We don't need to go there for anything. We have enough land and water here. Look at what was found there once!'

'A giant egg! And that poor man who picked up the huge egg, how he suffered after that! He lost his crops in a fire, his daughter went lame ... oh never, ever, forget all that!'

No one talked about the island and no one went

there. But today was different because it was time for an ADVENTURE!

Avani reached the shore, skipping nimbly over small rocks. It was lonely and deserted; she was still fearful, but she jumped and whooped.

'Great waters! I've done it! I've come alone to Bhoot Byet! That will show Delshad and Ambar, saying I was too terrified to come alone . . .'

She remembered the conversation she had had with Tavishi and the boys a few days earlier. Bored with their games, they had been flipping stones aimlessly across the pond. As usual it had become a contest and Avani said in disgust, 'You boys are useless, you never think of anything exciting. I have to think of things to do all the time.'

'You wouldn't dare to do what we think of,' Ambar had replied.

'Of course I would, you just can't think of anything good enough to scare me,' Avani had said, tossing her head.

'Okay then,' exclaimed naughty Ambar. 'We dare you to go to Bhoot Byet . . . alone. Tavishi won't go with you. Let's see now!'

Both boys had fallen about laughing.

'You DARE me to go? DARE?' returned Avani recklessly. 'As if I am scared. I never ignore a dare. I'll go, and I won't even tell you when!'

And here she was. Avani's brown eyes shone with mischief. She thought, They are the ones who are scared! They have never even tried to come, they only talk. She was jubilant as she thought of what she had managed to do.

Twelve-year-old Avani was lanky and tough. She and her group of three close friends played, squabbled and studied together in Bagasra. Their village was outside the small fortified town of Gola Dhoro, close to the placid Pavitra River, some distance from Lothal. It took only three to four days to reach Lothal by bullock cart, but was faster by riverboat. After all, it was 2570 BCE, and the only other way of going from place to place faster was on elephant-back, atop an ass or by sailboat.

Avani took a careful look at the long arm of land that extended to the river.

'Oh, it's quite big!' she realized. 'I should go and get proof that I have been here.'

So, looking around as she went, she made her way forward towards the copse of trees.

Srrr-srr-srr . . . she started at the rustling sound. It could be a scorpion or a snake!

'Be very careful,' she told herself. 'You don't want a scorpion sting!' But it was just a bandicoot skittering away. Avani heaved a sigh of relief. Thank the heavens there were no anthills either!

The sun was bright. Oh, the island feels so safe and ordinary, she thought, as she reached a wooded area.

As if to spite her, a breeze sprang up and in a few minutes became a whistling wind. She saw dark clouds above and rushed to shelter near some shrubs as the rain started. What a downpour! She looked sadly at her wet sari. However, her red clay bangles were okay, and her white shell hairclasps were still in place. At least she hadn't lost those. She was always getting scolded for losing things.

Within five minutes, the shower ceased. It was suddenly eerily silent. Avani shivered. The scene now was different. Everything was wet and soggy, and the river was flowing faster. She ran back to the raft, scared. She just wanted to get home now—the formerly friendly island seemed faintly menacing, deserted and quiet except for some small sounds.

Avani decided to get on the raft and return to the village as fast as she could. She reached the tree with its funny jutting-out branch near which she had moored the raft.

As she reached the rocks, she stopped, shocked.

There was no raft there.

Nor was there one floating nearby.

In fact, there was no raft anywhere at all, not even in the far distance!

Only water all around.

She was marooned!

3

RELIEF!

Avani looked around with narrowed eyes but all she could see was the river that flowed faster than ever. There was no way to get home!

No one knew she was here. She hadn't even told her best friend, eleven-year-old Tavishi. Avani was absolutely alone on Bhoot Byet and the heavenly skies alone knew what evil spirits and other scary things lived on it. In the wooded parts there would be boars and wolves; she just knew it. Her imagination ran wild and she remembered all the tales she had heard of elephants and tigers and lions . . .

She wanted to scream, 'Someone come and help me! Help!' But she knew it would be useless as there was no one around.

'I must be calm, I must be calm,' she repeated to herself. 'Breathe slowly and think . . .'

She stretched out her hands and prayed, 'Oh Mother River, oh goddess of water, come to my aid, I need your help. Guide me, guide me!'

Help would come eventually. Only, she feared it would be later rather than sooner. After all, she had done something forbidden. She had taken the raft out alone, and no one would think of looking for her by the riverside.

Maybe the boys would guess and tell someone! But when would they come? Would they be on time?

She sat up straight. What nonsense was this? Since when had she become so timid and helpless?

Action. That was what was needed, not sitting and wringing her hands. She would act, and NOW. She decided to climb the tree first, check her bearings and then figure out a plan. Once she had decided on that, she felt much better. It was always good to do something instead of waiting.

She'd find a way back home!

***

Avani walked over the smaller rocks till she reached some trees. She quickly tucked in one end of her short saree at the waist, so her arms and hands were free to climb up a tall tree. Finding a nice broad branch, she sat on it and looked around. Trees, a bit of river and some hillocks, and yet more trees in the distance. The island was much bigger than it had appeared from afar. She couldn't see the other side.

Suddenly she gave a yell of pure relief. A boat!

'Here, here, h-e-r-e!' she shouted and waved.

Someone waved a flat paddle back and continued in her direction. She got down and ran to the river bank, towards the rocks.

As the boat came closer, she gave another scream of disbelief. Tavishi! Alone! Timid but loyal Tavishi, who didn't even like to sit alone in a boat, forget paddling it! But underlying her fearfulness was a streak of naughtiness, which got full rein when she was with her friends.

Tavishi paddled hard, pushing her brown plait behind her, and threw a rope around a rock, getting it right in the first try. Avani practically skipped to the boat, feeling excited and relieved.

'Oh Tavishi, thank you . . . thank you so much . . . the raft floated away,' she explained, breathless, having stumbled and almost fallen.

'Let's go before everyone wonders where we are, or notices the boat missing,' said Tavishi.

'But how did you think of coming here?' Avani wanted to know.

'I saw you weren't around and searched everywhere. Went to the ancient ghat, saw your father's old raft was missing. Then I remembered that dare the boys gave you, realized what you had done and got worried.'

The two paddled hard, steering where required. They were good swimmers, having learnt in the pond and river at home, and had become strong with all the physical work they did. They swiftly crossed to the other side of the river.

'You came for me, Tavishi? But you hate paddling alone!' Avani exclaimed.

In reply she got a huge grin. 'Avani, I've lost my fear of being alone in a boat. I had no time to be scared or worry and when I settled down, I realized that I like the feeling of being alone on the water. It's so calm and beautiful! I saw three hamlets, I saw blue kingfishers . . . oh, it was lovely! So in a way, it's thanks to you.'

Avani then described the island, excited, brown eyes shining.

As they neared their village, they saw their friend, stocky Delshad in his short robe, pale-brown hair flopping on his forehead, standing by the riverside. Younger than them but sensitive by nature, he was quickly aware of anyone's happiness or misery. He lived up to his name, which meant 'one with a happy heart'. He and his sister Rubada had been orphaned when they were very young, but a kind clan member had adopted them. Delshad tried to keep the peace amongst his friends, so parents were always happy when he was around.

'Take me too!' he called out.

Avani was so thrilled about the mission being accomplished that she obliged. Delshad got in, his face split by a wide grin, green eyes shining, asking a hundred questions.

'I did it!' boasted Avani, very pleased with herself.

She said nothing of how scared she had been, though. Oh no, that was not for his ears!

'The island is much bigger than we had thought,' she continued. 'And it's very mysterious; there are hills and lots of trees . . . it's sort of sinister.' Here Avani lowered her voice; she loved drama!

'We must go there together. We'll have fun and it will be our secret,' she told the others.

'What happened to the raft? You'll get into trouble if your baba finds out where you were,' warned Delshad.

'Well, make sure he doesn't, then,' she replied with an apprehensive look on her normally sunny face.

Yes, she'd be in trouble if anyone knew she had gone alone. And Tavishi would be in trouble too, for going by herself to get her.

By then, they were nearly home. Bagasra!

Both girls touched the clay amulets, with a unicorn and mottled jasper gemstone on each, which they wore on a black thread around their necks. They also bowed their heads in a silent prayer of gratitude.

'Let's not mention the island at all, or we won't be allowed there again,' said Avani in an urgent tone.

'But have you seen yourself, Avani?' Tavishi asked, grinning. 'Your hair is wet, bedraggled . . . it's got bark stuck in it. And your saree! Your mother is going to . . .'

'Yes, I know,' interrupted Avani, looking ruefully at her knee-length dark red saree, made of coarse cotton. It was torn and damp and looked like a rag. Her blouse, which her mother had made by knotting a cloth at the back, and also at the waist to prevent scrapes and insect bites, was of a lighter colour and now had grass stains, mud stains and some purple marks on it. 'She is really going to be exasperated. She'll make me wash my clothes till I get the stains off!'

Tavishi, in comparison, looked so dainty and tidy. Avani's mother would be sure to point that out too! Tavishi liked to be neat, loved clips and bangles and was careful with them. She wore her saree without a blouse and was more sedate, so she didn't get hurt so often.

They continued paddling till they were at Bagasra Ghat, where the boat would be moored. Anyone coming

would think all three had been together, so Avani felt a little better.

'Please, let my father not know,' she prayed silently.

Just then they heard a shout.

'Avani! Wait!'

It was Avani's father. And wait they did. Angry fathers are not known for patience.

A tall, fair man with black hair, wearing a short dhoti, came striding up. His normally kind, open face now looked grim.

'Who took my raft? The truth please. Do you know why I kept it at the other ghat? Because it's old and needed repairing!' he asked sternly.

'Baba, I took it,' gulped Avani.

'Avani! I thought so. I don't want to hear a word. I saw

the raft was missing . . . and don't say you thought it didn't matter because it was the old one. AND you went alone. No, I don't want to hear any excuses, understood? You have broken the strictest rule by going out alone on the river. Now tell me, what's happened to my raft?'

'Baba-I-I . . . it floated away . . .' stammered Avani, in tears.

'Exactly! I had kept it tied to the ruined ghat for a reason. The rope was worn out and the raft needed repairs. I had not forgotten about it.'

Baba was in a rage, unusual for him, and not a pleasant person right then.

'I have scolded you time and time again for being impetuous and reckless. You just don't think!

'You are not allowed on the river alone, you know that. Never. For any reason. We have told you it can be dangerous if there is a sudden shower, or if you lose a paddle. We are lucky there are no gharial here. I'm sure you took my good bronze hook as well as the rope, and have lost them. Well, you are going to get punished.'

Avani swallowed hard, trying not to cry, though tears were not far away. Her father turned to the other two children. 'And you, Tavishi and Delshad, it's good you got her. Go home.'

But he was not finished with Avani yet. 'Avani, you will not go with us to the special haat this time. Stay at home and help look after the younger village children. And my word is final,' he said sternly.

Avani was shocked. 'Baba! You don't mean the grand bazaar? But there will be things which I've never seen from far-off towns and—'

'I said "no", Avani,' her father replied.

Avani's fate was decided; no treat for her. No more scolding, no questions, just this punishment. She was glad of at least one thing—Tavishi had not been caught. Otherwise she would have been in trouble as well for going alone, even if it was to rescue Avani. They would have to confess sometime. But not when Baba was so angry. Tavishi's father was more lenient . . . lucky her!

They reached home, Avani not uttering a single word. Her mother was there, along with Tavishi's, both wearing sarees wound around their bodies without blouses. They started scolding and questioning Avani. 'Why are you so wet? You will catch a cold! Look at your clothes! Where were you? Go and change!' they ordered, without waiting for any answers.

Later, Avani, wearing clean, dry clothes, quickly put rush mats on the floor for everyone to sit on, as they would all eat together. She placed the clay plates and bowls while her mother made rotis. They then had a lovely lunch of lentil curry, rotis, yoghurt and spicy vegetable pickle.

After lunch was cleared away and her father seemed to be in a better mood, Avani tried once more, 'Baba! Please may I go to the haat? I'll accept any other punishment! Everyone is going . . .'

'And everyone did not disobey their parents,' Baba replied. 'My child, I am sorry, but I have to teach you a lesson for your own good. The answer is no.'

Sulking, Avani went off to meet Tavishi, Delshad and Ambar under an old, gnarled mango tree. This year it had flowered profusely, so they were well-hidden, especially from the little ones.

'Hey, Avani, that was great,' said twelve-year-old Ambar with a wink. 'We didn't think you'd be able to do it. And how did you manage to come out now?'

Strong, hard-working and light-hearted, Ambar had sharp features and short dark hair, like his ancestors from the north. He was wearing a short tunic instead of the usual *langot* as he was recovering from a cold.

'Ma let me come. And Baba has not asked me where I went yet, so it's still our secret,' answered a greatly relieved Avani. 'Let's keep it that way. I don't want anyone to expressly forbid us from going to Bhoot Byet . . . then we really won't be able to go.

'Let's plan a picnic. And from now on, I will be so good, really, really good . . .'

At that everyone shrieked with laughter.

4

BAGASRA VILLAGE

Bagasra was large for a farming village. It was right next to the town of Gola Dhoro. People from different places, tribes and clans had settled there, thanks to the fertile soil and plenty of water brought by flooding rivers.

Delshad's ancestors were from far-off Persia, having come in stages over land to Meluhha, through the Bolan and Khyber passes. Tavishi's people were from the south; her great-great-grandparents had come by boat to Lothal and then travelled inland to Gola Dhoro, where they had finally settled. Avani's ancestors were from the hills or ghats along the western coast. Each clan had brought its language, traditions and customs, so there was an intermingling of cultures in the village. Tavishi used a Tamil dialect at home. But all of them understood and spoke the common language of Gola Dhoro.

Bagasra had fields, woods and ponds, where various birds could be found. Ambar, a keen birdwatcher, would be thrilled to see them, specially the migratory birds from the icy wastelands of the north.

The children of Bagasra village were a big, carefree group, but Avani, Tavishi, Delshad and Ambar were especially close. Every morning, sitting by the river, each child had to chant clan prayers to the sun, wind, water, fire and earth. Collecting firewood, helping in the fields, washing clothes and looking after the little ones were part of their chores. The girls also had to collect the 'mosquito plant' stems to keep away mosquitoes. The rest of the time was spent playing, swimming, practising with bows and arrows, and what their parents called 'running wild'!

One game the children loved was *saagargotte*. In this the smooth, round dried seeds of the wild yellow arali flower were thrown and caught in a flat, open palm, and the winner was the one who could hold all eight seeds at one time.

They would use sticks and practise drawing animals on the sand—from a zebu bull to an antelope or a tiger—all the pictures they saw etched on the seals. They also learnt to add and subtract, using river pebbles. Yes, they were a busy lot!

***

Three weeks went by in a flash, and soon it was time for the big haat.

Avani, Tavishi and the others swung like monkeys from the soap nut tree the day before. They were done with their chores.

'So tomorrow you people are going to the bazaar? Lucky you!' said Avani wistfully. She felt envious for a while, then grinned, thinking, I have to pay a price for going to

Bhoot Byet! What fun we'll have when all four of us go together! We must plan it properly.

She hugged herself in anticipation. She made herself think and plan only of Bhoot Byet; that way she wouldn't feel so bad about not going to the special haat.

Early next morning, a chirpy voice was heard outside Tavishi's house. 'Tavishi! Aren't you ready? You have to go with me, as your mother isn't coming.' The voice belonged to Ketika, the Village Elder's daughter and Avani's close friend. Ketika was tall and lithe, and good at all outdoor jobs. Her long, glossy hair was neatly tied, and she had black eyes that sparkled with humour. She was vivacious and kind, so everyone was very attached to her. But she was soon to be married, so she no longer played with Avani and her friends as much as she used to. She was given more grown-up chores to do now!

Everyone was getting ready to leave for the grand bazaar with their parents, except for Avani. Ketika looked at her sympathetically . . . it was really horrid to be left out like this. But she knew Avani's baba would never change the punishment. Avani, too, looked on, feeling miserable as ox-carts laden with various commodities like grain and dried fish passed by. Some people had loaded their goods on donkeys. People in Bagasra 'bought' things by exchanging them with other goods, so on market day, a peculiar variety of items was taken to be bartered. Some wild jungle fowl, dried fish, vegetables, fruit from the jungle . . . the list was endless.

After an hour of brisk walking the villagers reached another big village. It was called Mayurnagar because of the many peacocks around it. In a corner of a maidan, amidst a cluster of neem trees, was the bazaar. How the children of Bagasra village gaped! It was far bigger than any haat they had ever seen.

On one side were tethered the various animals who had carried goods. Herbs, leaves, roots and dried berries for medicinal uses were kept in neat piles under a tree. Another corner in the shade had lengths of coloured cloth hanging from trees. They swayed in the slight breeze and made a splash of colour above the ground that was set with all things dear to girls' hearts. Blouses for the cold winter mornings and beautiful shawls made of cotton and sheep's wool were attractively laid out.

Ribbons, bangles, earrings, rouge, kajal, lip colour, perfume jars and clips and pins were all fanned out. There was so much to see and choose from! Dhotis for the men, *langots*, coarse everyday cloth, fine woven cloth, coloured cloth with borders in a different colour, amulets made of different materials, like gemstones and terracotta...

A big area was reserved solely for different clay vessels, such as black vases with red designs on them, and huge bins for storage. There were terracotta toys as well, much to the delight of Tavishi, and shiny faience rams and bulls, which appealed to the younger children, along with lovely wooden whistles in animal shapes.

There was hustle and bustle everywhere—women bargaining, vendors haggling, voices calling, people shouting out their wares . . .

Tavishi at once tried her hand at bartering the reed baskets she had brought for the whistles, one for Avani and one for herself. Ketika was amused and helped her, showing her what to say and do. Ketika's mother, in the meantime, was bargaining with a woman for some bright-coloured cloth.

A stall of merchandise from Lothal! A ship had docked in from Mesopotamia, and a trader had brought the much-prized blue lapis lazuli stones used in jewellery. He was bartering these for spices, like peppercorns, and fine muslin cloth, which would go to Egypt from there. Ketika's mother rushed to the stall as soon as she heard about it. She called Ketika as well, who smiled and greeted the trader in the traditional manner, hands extended, palms open and head bowed low. The open palms signified that the person carried no hidden weapons, and the bent head showed respect. Eyes shining with excitement, Ketika said, 'Please, dada, may I hold them just once, they are so beautiful!'

'Yes, my child, but be very careful,' he replied, smiling kindly, understanding Ketika's thrill at handling them.

Ketika's mother managed to bargain for a small fistful of

lapis lazuli, giving the trader finely spun cotton, amongst other things, in exchange. She would get these stones made into a beautiful necklace for her daughter, interspersed with local green stones.

She then went to a stall displaying pearls from Dilmun. Everyone was ooh-ing and aah-ing over them, but only a few people had anything of great or unusual value to barter for them. A few merchants had come from Mohenjo daro just for this haat, and they were bargaining away, for they had Harappan goods prized in other lands. Tavishi and Ketika looked on in wonder—milky white pearls, grey pearls, each lustrous, mysterious and beautiful. Ketika's mother had to haggle hard, as she certainly wanted these for her daughter.

Meanwhile, Ambar and Delshad were having a grand time looking at the different farming implements. There were axles, spades, stone and metal drills, weights made of chert rock in cuboid shapes, famous the world over as they were so accurate. Metal tools for etching could be seen too. The variety was mind-boggling!

The grown-ups were more interested in commodities like live fowl, vegetables and grain, which the children didn't care for. They couldn't wait to tell Avani about this haat! Tired after all the running around, they finished eating and got ready to return to their village.

***

Meanwhile, back home in Bagasra . . .

'Avani, look after the younger children. I won't be able to run after them; we are grinding wheat. And take care, remember you are the eldest and don't behave foolishly. No doing crazy things,' cautioned her mother, cleaning the round, flat stone for grinding grain. She was always busy, looking after the children and the home. Her small frame belied her strength and skill at shooting. Everyone in the village had learned to use bows, to throw stones and spears, to protect themselves from any animal that ventured close.

Avani sighed. She liked playing when she wanted to, not when she was told to!

'Hey, Rubada, Nadeesh, stop fighting over that! Come, we'll play hide-and-seek with the others,' she called the children, who were tugging at a toy monkey that moved on a string.

Though impatient by nature, Avani was very fond of children. She had lost a baby sister a few years earlier, and missed her. Babies had to be carefully looked after, specially when they had a fever, for illness was swift and often cruel. This was something dinned into the children as they grew older.

It was Avani's turn to hide first. She managed to climb and hide herself in the old mango tree. She soon heard shouts of, 'Avvvaneeee Tai! Avani Tai! Where are you?' Then she heard, 'Oh, maybe she has gone near the brick kiln . . . let's go there.'

They scampered off. Avani grinned. It would take the children ages to reach the kiln, it was so far. She could climb down and be safe for a while, till they returned!

She was about to start climbing down when two men came and sat against the tree trunk, looking hot and tired.

'Thank heavens for a bit of shade,' said one, his voice floating up quite clearly.

'We deserve it,' replied the other.

Avani's eyes widened. Who were they? She didn't know them. And she knew everyone in Bagasra. In fact, everyone knew everyone in the village! Strangers? Probably traders. That was always a source of excitement.

Both men had beards, and wore robes and turbans, like most traders. Turbans covered their faces and protected them from dust during journeys, kept their heads protected from the heat in summer and also kept their ears warm in winter. Their accent was different from that of anyone she knew. She could hear them as she was not very high up, though well-hidden.

The first one had a peculiar nasal tone. He said, 'It's good you found out about today's big bazaar. The men have gone, and most of the families . . . we'd never have got a better day. No one will return soon. And no locked doors here, either.'

'Yes, foolish people! They trust everyone,' replied the other, clearing his throat with a gruff sound.

'All the better for us. There will be trouble for these people sometime. And serve them right; these Harappans think they are so clever. How they have troubled me . . .'

Avani couldn't help listening. Something was very strange here. What were they planning? Why were they so mean about her people? She HAD to know more.

'Let's take a look at the stuff we've got,' said the one with a bad throat.

'They are so stupid! An Elder's house and no guards, only barking dogs . . . who ran off when we threw stones at them,' sneered the nasal-voiced man, who had shaggy eyebrows and a reddish beard. He was wearing a badly-dyed, dirty green turban.

Avani realized that they were talking about Ketika's house. That was the only Elder's house which was empty. What had they done?

The men were examining some objects now. Avani's eyes popped out as she saw them. Why, she was sure that one was a mirror. Very few people had mirrors in Bagasra . . .

She strained her ears as they murmured softly, heads bent. In the mixture of languages, she could hear one word clearly: Ketika. The mirror and a wooden box, they looked like Ketika's. Were these men thieves? Did they know Ketika? Although frightened, she kept listening, trying to find out more.

The men lifted their heads and their words could be heard more clearly.

'I've kept it at the old landing stage,' the gruff-voiced man said.

They looked scary and unpleasant, but Avani was avid to hear more, to understand what this was all about. Quietly and very slowly, she slithered down. Suddenly one of her plaits caught on a branch. She managed to free her hair, but in her eagerness and haste, she missed a foothold and went crashing down.

She looked up at an angry face.

'Spying on us, were you? I'll show you what we do to little girls like you!' the nasal-voiced, bearded man growled.

His red flowing beard, long tunic and ferocious scowl added to Avani's terror.

'No sir, no, I-I wasn't spying,' she stammered. 'We were playing hide-and-seek and I was just hiding . . .'

The other man was nowhere to be seen.

'Tell me, what did you hear?' The man's voice was soft and curt, terrifying, and sent a chill down her spine.

'N-n-n-no-nothing,' she stammered again.

'Then go, find your friends, or things will be worse for you,' he replied, pulling her up from the ground.

Twisting out of his grip, Avani ran as fast as she could. She didn't stop anywhere, just kept running. All of a sudden she tripped as she neared the long field. Gasping for breath, she lay on the ground. Had anyone followed her? If she got up, would one of those horrible men catch her? She looked behind her cautiously . . . no one. She was safe. She sat up, rubbing her knees, not noticing one badly grazed elbow.

The younger children were already home. They had got tired of looking for her.

Avani didn't know what to do. She decided to wait till the others came home—she had to tell them what had happened!

When her friends returned they all talked together at once, interrupting each other. Tavishi, Ambar and Delshad were busy describing the bazaar, but when Avani told them about the men, they listened, looking a bit scared.

'I was petrified,' admitted Avani, who shuddered when she thought of the man who had threatened her. 'He looked so scary, although he had a funny voice . . .'

'Maybe they are bad people. Let's keep a lookout for them,' said Tavishi.

'Let's go to the next village tomorrow and search,' suggested Avani.

'No, we'll get into trouble,' warned a troubled Delshad.

But at Avani's insistence, they went searching the next day. They looked everywhere, but spotted no strangers. Disappointed, they were on their way back, when Avani clutched Ambar. 'There he is, I tell you, look!' A red-bearded man in a robe was walking ahead briskly.

The children quietly followed him a long way, hiding behind rocks and bushes if he changed direction. After a while, as they were hiding, he went out of sight. They emerged from their hiding place, behind two trees. Just then, Ambar's robe was grabbed from behind and he was swung around, to face the irate man they were following. But he was not the red-bearded man Avani had encountered!

'You rude children! Following me, making fun of me, were you? I will tell your parents!' he barked at them.

'Pardon us, we are sorry,' stammered a red-faced Ambar, as they started backing away. The angry man let them go, but not before scolding them soundly, talking about manners and respect towards elders.

'You let us in for this, Avani. I'm never going to listen to you again!' exclaimed an upset, indignant Ambar.

'Avani, don't let your imagination run wild . . . there must be a perfectly good explanation for what you heard,' said peace-loving Delshad. And that was the end of it.

In the village there was no talk of Ketika's house being robbed, as nothing was found missing. Only a few terracotta toys lay near the Elder's hedge, and there were footmarks on the damp ground near the bushes. However, the small houses close to Ketika's had signs of someone having entered. Again, only a few toys were found thrown nearby and nothing was missing, so it was shrugged off as children's pranks.

But in her heart of hearts, Avani was not convinced . . .

5

BHOOT BYET

'Listen, if we really want to go to Bhoot Byet, let's be good, finish our chores and our parents will let us go easily enough,' suggested Avani the next day.

'Mind you don't do anything foolish,' added Tavishi with a wink. 'We don't want any punishments. I heard your parents say you were getting far too bold and it's not safe, Avani.'

'Yes, but it's so long ago that I took the raft ... they must have forgotten about it. And I have actually tried to be good all these days,' Avani replied.

'You really think they've forgotten?' asked Tavishi dubiously.

'Of course!' cried Avani, though inwardly she was anxious and uncertain.

The next week found all four of them doing their chores diligently.

Tavishi helped her mother decorate the walls of the house, drawing scenes of tigers and another of villagers dancing in a circle ...

Avani went to collect firewood . . .

Delshad repaired the fencing of a field with thorny dry shrubs, a task he hated. His father was very pleased with him!

Ambar worked with his father to prepare a channel for irrigating the distant fields. He was strong and worked fast and well, and was praised for his work.

'Baba, may we please go out in the boat? We will all go together. Delshad's and Ambar's parents have agreed! We want to have a picnic and do some fishing. Pl-eea-se!' wheedled Avani one day, when she saw her father in a good mood.

Baba agreed with a smile, tweaking her plait gently, only saying, 'Remember the rules!'

Avani smiled back at Baba, thinking, At least Baba is fair, once I am punished that is the end of the matter . . . not like Ma who keeps on reminding me of what I have done . . .

The children excitedly started planning their trip.

'Let's take the lovely fried *chivda* your mother makes, Avani,' Delshad suggested. All the children loved the various fried treats, which they got often, as ghee was plentiful.

'And sugarcane!' said Tavishi.

On the way the children sang songs, challenged each other with memory games, joked and had a great time.

Having been to the island once before, Avani decided where to cross the river. 'I crossed soon after passing our village, beyond where the other small river joins ours. The current on the other side is much gentler.'

They were soon going upriver on the smaller river, Aravali, which no one ever went on.

'There it is!' yelled Tavishi, pointing to the island in the far distance.

'Let's circle around. There may be a better place to get off,' suggested Delshad. So both boys continued paddling, till they went round the curve . . . only to find that there was no other suitable place to moor the boat. It was too full of reeds and water, trees and nesting water-birds . . . nothing like a sandy or rocky shore to tie up the boat. So they continued till they were back to where Avani had stopped. Drawing close, Avani passed the stunted tree, but this time they stopped at a sandier spot ahead, with more reeds. Avani moored the boat to a strong tree.

They walked up the sloping bank, slightly scared. What would they find?

Tavishi shivered; she did NOT like the island, but she wasn't going to say anything. Anyway, with the others around, it would be less frightening.

Avani proudly led the way, chattering nineteen to the dozen. With all four there, it was easy to talk of the good bits about the island, and her earlier fears seemed ridiculous.

'It's just a deserted island,' she said. 'Wonder why people left it? Maybe there weren't enough wells, or because it's rockier, so not many crops would grow . . . who knows!'

All of a sudden they heard ducks quacking. Where? There was nothing in sight.

'Ambar, it's you!' Avani realized. Ambar was famous for his perfect imitations of bird calls and had often fooled them. His eyes crinkled with laughter . . . this was fun!

'Everyone says this is a bad place, there are bad

spirits here. Remember the egg that was found? Very inauspicious,' added superstitious Tavishi, shuddering.

'Just listen to all those birds and the squirrels on the trees. What a racket they are making!' Ambar exclaimed.

'They'll drive out the bad spirits,' laughed Avani.

'Look, here's some dardi berry. Let's take some back, its juice is good for headaches,' called Ambar, the nature expert. 'Look, there's also a fever tree. Its flowers bring down fever. And here's an amla tree.'

Avani exclaimed with glee, 'See, we girls have our very own baskets! Not like you boys with only *langots*!' Gathering the amlas in her saree pallav, she tied it firmly into a bundle.

The children then discovered a copse of fruit trees, definitely planted by someone long ago. There were chikoos, half-eaten by birds, lying underfoot. The undergrowth was thick; some parts were thorny and other parts had tiny flowers. Dragonflies, and blue, green and yellow butterflies flew around, looking bright and beautiful. All was peaceful and sunny.

'This should be called Rainbow Island—it's so colourful! Look at those birds—green barbets, brown and white tree-pies, striped hoopoes and oh, these flowers and fruit!' Avani skipped as she exclaimed.

'See, ber!' said Delshad, his mouth full, eating even the sour green ones.

'I hope we find a *pulli* tree. I love tamarind,' said Tavishi and everyone laughed, remembering how one time she had got stuck on a tamarind tree branch, and Avani had had to help her down.

The children were surprised when they came upon a

small brick-lined well, just like the ones in their village. Even the top had bricks extending upwards.

'So people did live here,' said Ambar triumphantly. 'And it had been abandoned, because of bad luck ... something terrible must have happened.' He gave an exaggerated shiver, bent on frightening the girls.

'But there are no huts or small houses like ours,' interjected Avani.

'There are hillocks that side, let's go see them. We should climb up. This island is much bigger than it looked from the boat,' observed Delshad. 'Maybe we'll find something interesting there.'

Tavishi shivered. She said in a small voice, 'I keep thinking I'll see a spirit.' She sounded ashamed of her fear.

The boys winked at each other. Hey, this was a great chance to frighten her!

The girls were walking ahead when they heard eerie shrieks and moans.

'What's that?' Tavishi exclaimed.

'The bhoot of Bhoot Byet,' chortled a ghostly voice.

Both girls turned away in disgust.

The boys kept giggling as Ambar chanted, 'The ghosts of Ghost Island!' Then they danced around Avani and Tavishi.

'At least you should have had the brains to do this after sometime . . . we knew it was you,' said Avani. 'You didn't even try to change your voice.'

The girls turned their backs on Ambar and Delshad and walked on.

'Lovely flowers! Such a pretty purple! exclaimed Tavishi, squirming at getting scared and changing the topic.

After a while the girls heard a yell.

'Where are Ambar and Delshad? They were right behind us,' Avani wondered.

'Up a tree, waiting for us to come so they can throw fruit on us?' asked Tavishi. They were used to the practical jokes played by the boys all the time.

'But we've been walking for more than five minutes, so we are quite far . . . maybe they went in the opposite direction,' said Avani. 'They're playing the fool as usual . . . just being idiotic, hiding from us.'

They continued walking and again heard a faint call.

'We'd better go see what's wrong,' sighed Avani. 'Let's turn around.'

They retraced their steps till they heard Ambar's voice coming further from the left. It sounded urgent and a little frightened.

'Hurry . . . I think they are in trouble!' said Avani, and the girls ran.

6

SECRETS OF BHOOT BYET

The girls kept looking around as they ran, but could see no sign of either Ambar or Delshad.

'Just keep track of where we are going. I don't want to get lost,' said Tavishi.

'Help!' came Ambar's voice again, sounding urgent. It definitely seemed closer.

'It's coming from underground. What on earth?' wondered Avani aloud.

And yes, the voice did seem to be coming from under them . . . from a ditch, roundish in shape. It was covered with dried leaves and old branches, so if one didn't watch out, one could easily walk into it.

Which the boys had done.

Smart guys!

After they had removed the leaves, the girls could see both the boys, dried twigs in their hair, mud around them, dusting themselves. The ditch was quite deep.

'Don't come any closer,' called Delshad.

'It's dark and dingy,' warned Ambar.

It was a pit that had been dug many, many years ago. The girls lay down on their stomachs, throwing out rotten branches. Once they had cleared the top, the boys could see them. They described how they had both walked straight into the pit, and were bruised.

'Now get a branch, a strong one, mind, so that we can get a grip,' yelled Ambar.

Avani found one and pushed it down.

'Eeks! Be careful, there may be a snakes' nest. Though we checked the pit, you never know what will come out from where!' cautioned Ambar.

Both Ambar and Delshad were lying on a pile of old leaves, which had sunk under their weight.

'It's not really *that* deep,' remarked Delshad, relieved now that help was at hand.

The boys positioned the branch at an angle till it reached the top, and Delshad held it while the taller Ambar slowly climbed out. Then he found a stronger branch and placed it for Delshad to climb out. Both looked a bit shaken, dirty and scratched, but were not badly hurt.

'It happened so suddenly, without warning. One minute we were fooling around, next we were falling inside. We tried to get out, but there were some thorny branches, and they really hurt,' Delshad described breathlessly.

They dusted off the dried leaves and mud, sitting in the shade of a tree.

'It's a pit made by people . . . no ghosts, Tavishi, sorry to disappoint you!' Ambar grinned.

The boys felt better after eating some fruit and looked around.

People had lived here. Though neglected, there were

still vegetables growing wild—large gourds and pumpkins that had obviously been planted by someone. There was a patch of herbs and medicinal plants, a shell-plant used for malaria that they recognized instantly and cow-grass, which helped to ease stomach aches.

'See, here's the proof . . . maybe they are like those people your grandfather told us about, Ambar, the ones who used to live in pits in winter in the mountainous north, to keep warm.'

Delshad's imagination was running wild. 'I think I saw something like a *chulah* too. Maybe a fugitive hid here?'

'Rubbish! It was so dark, you couldn't see anything. You're imagining it,' scoffed Ambar. 'And anyway, how could someone get in and out of the pit?'

'Maybe they have steps cut into the side. That is what old Thatha told us once. The people stayed down there to protect themselves against wild animals and the cold,' Delshad persisted with his theory.

Each one of them remembered bits from the tales told by the oldest man in the village, whom they all called Thatha. He had wispy white hair and a surprisingly long moustache.

'We have to explore this place further . . . it's so intriguing,' Avani jumped up. 'Let's go!' All four were in total agreement and got up fast.

The only things of interest they found were the beginnings of three tiny huts with low brick walls, and nothing else. The children were disappointed, as they had hoped to find a few ruined houses at least . . . proof that people had lived there.

'We have to see the hillocks too . . .' Ambar remembered.

Avani said slowly, 'If we get late, Baba will want to know what happened, where we were . . . Let's forget the hillocks, let's just look at them from here and then go back home.'

'Actually, yes,' agreed Delshad, wrinkling his brow. 'I remember seeing Avani's baba that day when Avani had come alone to Bhoot Byet, and he was wild.'

They walked some more and looked at the hilly area, which was completely surrounded by trees. Yet, on the left, there was a dark patch . . . certainly caves! Excited, they made wild guesses and spent a few minutes wondering what they'd find if they explored them.

'Oh-oh-oh . . . Another egg? Animals? Lizards? Owls? Bats? Eeks . . . forget it,' shrieked Tavishi.

Reluctantly they turned around, deaf to the pleas of Ambar, who wanted to carry on ahead, and Tavishi, who prudently wanted Avani to enter first.

'Another day,' promised Avani. 'We'll go straight there. We've been all round the island. Then the way you two stupidly fell took up a lot of our time. Now we have to find some fish before we go back . . .'

They left. And they did manage to find fish to take home.

The next day, when the children were free from their chores, they discussed Bhoot Byet at length. The fact that only they knew about it made it a mysterious, lonely island, full of promise of exciting things.

'We have to go there again soon,' Avani decided and the others agreed, each imagining dangerous adventures, remembering all the stories they had heard around the fire at night.

As they were about to go home, Avani thought she heard the crackle of dry twigs and looked around. There were some bushes behind their favourite mango tree, but she couldn't see anyone, though she looked hard.

Those silly children, always after us, trying to find out what we do, what we talk about, she thought. 'Shoo, go away, shoo, or come out and show yourselves,' she called.

But it was no child. A grown man had been skulking around, wanting to know where they had been. And yes, he knew their secret . . . He melted into the distance . . .

7

GOLA DHORO

A few days later, Avani raced through her chores and ran to Tavishi's house. When she got there, she discovered that Tavishi was in trouble. She had run out to play with their friends Gatita, Vanhi and Sarasi without telling her mother, and was getting a good talking-to.

'Tavishi, why haven't you done your chores? No going off to play till I say so. Now hurry and finish!' her mother scolded.

Hearing all this, Avani slunk away. She'd be alone today! How boring! She felt disgruntled, as she had nothing planned, and wandered around. Then she brightened up. She'd go to the Big Wall, the fortification wall which surrounded the town of Gola Dhoro. Just inside the barricade were workshops; sheds for storing stock to be sent to other places; storerooms to keep wheat, dried peas, barley; and some wealthy merchants' houses, decorated with carved wooden boards. Broad and orange in the sunlight, it always looked exciting to her because she didn't live inside that citadel. However, the children often went there and knew many of the people inside.

Avani walked to the three-metre-wide sheesham wood signboard with the name 'Gola Dhoro' written on stone in the Harappan script. She then went to the north-west side of the wall and climbed the steps, smiling at the guards there. Sesame fields bordered this gate. She knew where the different workshops were and enjoyed watching the craftsmen at work, whenever they allowed her to stay, that is.

Ah, here was a shell workshop, same as the one outside, a rectangular shed constructed of sun-baked bricks. Earrings and bangles were made there. She looked rueful . . . she'd broken her shell bangles only yesterday!

'Avani!' called one of the shell-cutters, who was sorting the shells. 'I've got some pink shells left over, want some?'

'Dada, may I have those to put on my wooden jewellery box, please? I want to make it the best one in the village, better than even Ketika's,' Avani replied.

'I'll make a brooch for you to wear for Ketika's wedding. I heard you got into trouble and couldn't go to the bazaar as punishment.' The shell-cutter smiled, his eyes twinkling. He, too, had often got into trouble at Avani's age and sympathized with her. She grinned at him as she sat watching two men cut conch shells with cutters. These shells had been brought from Nageshwar, on the coast of the Gulf of Kachh.

After a while she got up, saying, 'I want to see the new bead workshop on the southern side.' Once there, she sat watching quietly as a big oven was prepared for heating the stones collected from the riverbed. Flat clay cakes to retain the heat were stacked at the bottom. It took hours of heating for the stones kept in the jars and crucibles to change colour and turn red.

It's like magic—apply heat and ordinary-looking, yellowish-brown stones transform into these beautiful red carnelians from which lovely jewellery is made, she thought.

A worker was sorting the coloured baked beads by size and storing them in small jars. He gave a few rich red and some lighter red discarded beads to Avani.

'Dada! That's great! Thank you so much,' Avani said happily.

Next, he started chipping the stones to the required size. They would then go to the expert driller.

The driller was in a corner, making a hole through a bright-coloured stone so it could be threaded for a necklace. This was done with a tapered cylindrical drill made of chert.

He is so skilled, thought Avani as she looked on admiringly. How I'd love to do that!

Another worker was sitting further away, polishing the red stones with glittering white quartz dust to make them smooth and shiny. Near him were heavy stone querns and pestles to produce shiny quartz dust by grinding the little rocks.

Avani felt a sneeze coming up; the white powder had gone up her nose. She held her nose; she couldn't let a sneeze escape! Mihir Kaka, the polisher, had a bad temper. If she disturbed him, he'd shoo her out. Time to go!

Wait, there was something new there. What were those chunks of stone? Green-red-white? She asked the stone-sorter.

'That's variegated jasper-stone. We only store them here. They are made into brooches and necklaces at Mohenjo daro. There's also mottled black-and-white jasper—you know what that is for—we make beautiful lucky charms from those,' he told her.

'Thank you!' said Avani, glad to learn something new. 'I'm going now, Dada. I'll see you again later.'

She skipped out. What was she going to do now? The road was deserted and she was bored. She walked on, humming. Suddenly she looked up and stopped sharply in her tracks. There were two men near the old well! Men wearing robes, faces half–covered with the ends of their turbans. One had a reddish beard and his long patchy green turban trailed over one shoulder. Her heart thudding, she stood rigid, fearful. Was it those men? Was the red-beard the one who had shouted at her when she was playing hide-and-seek?

'Why am I so afraid? I'm not in danger here in Gola Dhoro . . . I can't be such a scared baby . . .' she told herself and waited, silent and alert.

She heard one of the men say in a nasal tone, 'I know a good place where we can wait, unseen and unsuspected. Come.'

They walked into an alleyway.

Avani followed at a distance, ready to run if need be.

The men entered a storeroom and pulled the door open.

Avani realized that the door was ajar and by pressing her ear to it, she could hear them. She overheard, 'Fire . . .' but not what followed. Straining her ears a little more, she further heard, 'We must wait, and only then can I go. It's important.'

Judging from the voices, they seemed to be the same men under the tree! She had never seen them again, but while the others had forgotten about them, she hadn't.

'Foolish people of Harappa. I will show them,' the nasal-voiced, red-bearded one continued. 'They punished me, put me in prison, just because I knocked out that man and stole his goats. Two goats! "Harappans do not tolerate violence," they said. I'll show them what we do!'

A rough voice replied, 'But they said they gave you a lenient punishment because you were a foreigner and didn't know the laws . . .'

'Hmph! Lenient!' the nasal-voiced man snapped. 'What do they think? Will I ever forget the work I was made to do? Till fields, harvest grain, sow seeds, carry water, dig canals to carry water to the fields from the river . . . so humiliating, to be treated like a slave . . .'

Avani strained her ears for all she was worth, wondering if she should go for help or listen further. She stood rooted, praying that someone would pass by. She heard a laugh, then one of the men again cleared his throat in a peculiar manner.

The gruff-voiced one said, 'We'll go away once we see it. You have to carry out what we planned; don't forget, and make sure no one spots you. We will leave clues; let's see if these clever people can understand them. Once this is over, I will have all the power!'

'And Sonu, hahaha! Sonu will be . . .' The other man let out an evil, nasal laugh that sounded like a horse's neigh.

As she shifted her position, Avani caught a glimpse of the two turbaned men. They looked surly, although she could not see their full faces. Suddenly they looked up for a second, glanced, rather, glared around, as though they had heard something. Immediately, Avani tooks to her heels, running lightly as fast as could—she didn't want to get caught again.

Who were these people who kept appearing and disappearing?

The lane was deserted. Was anyone following her, she wondered fearfully, as she raced even faster. She would go home and tell Baba everything at once.

As she reached the end of the street, a bitter-sour smell suddenly hit her. Looking up, she saw a wisp of smoke curling somewhere ahead. In a flash she realized what it was. A fire!

8

FIRE

Avani ran through another small, narrow alley to get to the source of the smoke.

'Fire! Fire! Baba! Dada!' she yelled, terror in her voice. Wisps of smoke were escaping from under the locked door of the small granary in their village. Surplus grain was stored in there to be sent to Mohenjo daro for distribution. And from there, city-made articles were sent back to the village. At the time, corn and barley had been stored in the small granary. Luckily, the wheat had not yet been brought in, though it had been harvested.

'Fire!' she screamed at the top of her lungs.

There was a sudden burst of sounds. Running feet, shouts and yells—total pandemonium as people entered the scene. The smell of fire, sharp and suffocating, filled the air, as smoke and crackling sounds were heard. *Crraaashh* . . . The door was falling down. Yellow-orange flames were visible now.

The men swung into action. They formed a chain, with two men drawing water from a wealthy merchant's house-well and handing it to the others. Each man stood in his dhoti and cotton vest, passing clay jars, metal pots, anything that would hold water, as fast as it was filled, to the next person. The men from the fields were wearing only a loincloth, having come running as soon as they heard the word 'fire'. Hiroo dada, from the neighbouring village of Ranginapur, who had come to deliver something, was especially helpful. There was hectic activity. Avani also tried to help.

'Out of the way, Avani,' said one of the craftsmen roughly. 'This is no place for little girls.'

'Move, Avani, you're just getting in the way,' shouted another.

And everywhere, 'Go away . . . go, Avani, not now! Not now!'

Avani moved away as there was no chance of her being able to pass on even one jar of water.

The fire was soon under control. There were sighs of relief. Small groups of people watched from a distance. Women held on tightly to their children, not allowing them to squirm away to get a closer glimpse of the fire. Some people were just looking, mouths wide open, eyes round with fear, while others were whispering and pointing at the flames, which were now dying down. Fire in the grain storeroom was a calamity. All the hard work done by the farmers in the fields could have been wasted.

Thankfully, the fire was doused completely after sometime, but the talking and wondering aloud continued. How had the fire been caused? When did it start and who had been careless, and with what? Questions buzzed around, but there were no immediate answers.

Avani had got separated from the small groups and everyone had forgotten about her. She stood towards the rear, near the corner, and no one could see her.

All of a sudden she heard a small, scared mewing and looked around. No, it was coming from above. Looking up through the smoky haze, she saw a cat. A terrified cat, stuck in a brick cavity, who seemed unable to move. He stood, back arched, tail waving high in the air, hair on end . . . and the tail was puffed to twice its size. Avani started to cough due to the smoke, and when she looked up, the cat had vanished! No, he had moved further back, scared by Avani's coughing. He was stuck and could not budge.

I'll have to do something, she decided. Lucky no one can see me, or is interested in what I'm doing, else they'd have shooed me away!

'Just be patient, Maoo,' she called out to the cat.

The cat came out again. Avani thought fast.

'Good cat, come down,' she coaxed in a soft voice, hoping the animal would lose its fear. She talked soothingly, and the cat continued to look at her, tail held up. Crouching low, but looking directly at the cat, she kept up a series of soothing words and noises, at the same time looking around for something to help it. After a while she found an old, half-broken bamboo pole. She ran and heaved it up, stood it at an angle and pushed it near the brick cavity. The cat mewed again. He now seemed to be following what Avani was trying to do.

The cat climbed down the bamboo, stepping gingerly. The pole was old and weather-beaten, with many holes and scratches, so the cat got a good grip with his claws. But to Avani's great astonishment, midway, he ran UP the bamboo again. He jumped on the roof, and came down carefully, holding a small white kitten by the scruff of its neck! He left the kitten at Avani's feet, ran up again, and brought down a tiny black-and-white kitten. Then a third one was brought down!

Avani deftly knotted the end of her saree, forming a kind of bag, and gingerly picked up the kittens, putting them in it.

The cat had once more done the vanishing act . . . he was nowhere to be seen. He hadn't even looked at the kittens, just left them with Avani. He seemed to know they would be safe with her.

Avani walked slowly through another alley, her interest in the fire diverted by the kittens, who seemed to have bunched themselves into one big ball. She had something far better to do now.

On reaching home, her first thought was, I'll have to feed the kittens. They were petrified, and only mewed and curled into each other, spitting and hissing at her if she tried to move them from the little, old, woven reed basket she had placed them in. She then called her mother, who looked shocked on seeing her. 'Avani! Soot! Ashes! Your face and arms and legs . . . Black! Are you hurt or burnt anywhere?' she asked anxiously. 'Your saree is ripped!' she exclaimed, her forehead puckered with worry. Avani hastily told her everything and together they tried to feed the scared, angry kittens.

Soon, Avani's three friends also came over, responding to her yells. They had gone running to see the fire, and by the time they reached, Avani had gone home with the kittens.

'The cat was big . . . a huge fellow, with so many scars. It was orange in colour and had green eyes, but it was so gentle with the babies,' she said, telling them details of the fire as well. 'My mother told me that male cats are caring about kittens too.' Everyone was envious of her.

Then she remembered the two men and told the others what she had overheard.

Who were these men? How come they vanished and no one saw them?

This was a big question to which there was no answer.

9

MYSTERIOUS HAPPENINGS

Who could have been careless enough to cause the fire? There were no clues as to who had been there. In fact, except for a few clay toys, nothing had been found. It was truly puzzling.

The needle of suspicion pointed to Sonu, who carried and stored the surplus grain. However, when questioned, Sonu looked bewildered, scratching his head and insisting that he had checked the storeroom carefully before closing the door. 'I swear by the holy spirits that I would never be so careless. People could have starved because of this!' he said. 'It would be disrespecting all our hard work. No, had I been responsible, I would have confessed and shown my repentance.' He sounded sincere, but the seeds of doubt had been sown in everyone's minds.

No one could understand the cause of the fire either. The headman of Gola Dhoro said, 'It looks like we will have to keep guard on even the locked stores, so that vandals cannot do any harm.'

The consequences of the fire were not as bad as

they had feared. They would have to repair the grain storeroom, and clean the soot and scorch marks. Some of the sacks had got burnt, some grain was destroyed and the soft steatite seals used as labels had been baked hard in the heat of the fire. These seals were important, because the tiny pictograms on them represented the names of the merchants and families to whom they belonged.

A rare, important seal belonging to an important merchant was missing. It was a tiny rectangular box with a sliding cover, which could be tied to a sack.

The hero of the day, Hiroo, was thanked by all and warmly invited for Ketaki's wedding. Avani also got her share of praise for keeping her head and calling people instead of running away. Her baba was proud of her, and so was Ma. Praise for Avani was music particularly to her mother's ears, as she usually only got to hear of her daughter's harum-scarum ways, so different from some of the docile girls she knew, who didn't lose things, or come home with their saree ends stained dark with purple jamun juice, or with tangled, wild hair hanging down their backs!

Avani's friends started teasing her, because ever since the fire, the orange cat, which Avani had named Manimaoo Babu, would appear out of nowhere and start walking beside her ... the cat had adopted her! He'd rub himself affectionately against her leg and look at her with unblinking eyes, which seemed to shine. He came and went on his own terms. If Avani called him and he didn't want to go with her, he would ignore her and stroll away, or groom himself, or just sit and look disdainful. Tavishi called him 'the cat who walks alone'. The kittens had disappeared the night of the fire and unlike the cat, never reappeared.

The days went by swiftly, and Avani and Tavishi made plans to go to Bhoot Byet once more, along with the boys. There was a lot of work though, for Ketika's wedding was coming up and preparations had started. Avani knew she had to be on her toes, finish helping in the house and do some outside chores, only then would she be free. It was the same with the others.

One day when she went to the shed attached to the buffalo shed for some dung-cakes for fuel, she heard small pebbles falling, as though someone had slipped on them. She turned around sharply and thought she saw the edge of a long cloth ... someone's turban! Ignoring it, she went inside, only to hear the door being slammed shut behind her. She pushed the door, but someone had shut it from the outside . . . the wooden bar was down! One of the children, she thought, irritated. They will be back in a few minutes, then I'll show them.

She finished her work and got ready to leave. But the door still wouldn't budge. She checked again and again. Now Avani was scared. She should have heard some giggles from the children outside, but there was only silence. A horrible, lonely hour went by . . . to her it felt like a year. Then finally she heard a noise outside, and her heart started thudding. Fear was uppermost in her mind, but there was anger too. Just let her catch whoever had shut her in!

The door was pushed open unceremoniously after a short time. It was Tavishi, who had been sent to look for her.

'What have you been doing here so long? Why didn't you come back home? Your baba is so irritated, he has been waiting for you,' Tavishi said as soon as she came in.

'I couldn't, Tavishi, the door was closed—' Avani stopped mid-sentence as she saw Tavishi's expression.

'Avani, the door was not barred when I came. It was just stuck; you must have imagined it was latched,' she said.

Avani knew she hadn't. She was certain she hadn't been mistaken. The door had been shut so tight that it wouldn't move an inch.

'No chance of going to Bhoot Byet tomorrow. I dare not ask Baba now, not after I delayed when he had told me to hurry,' she said, looking glum. 'It's a mystery . . . I know it was locked. Someone must have come and opened it later.'

Both the girls looked at each other. Avani had a great sense of foreboding; something was wrong somewhere.

They went home quietly. 'Why are you so late? You are always dreaming! This is not the time for that, there is so much work,' Avani's mother grumbled. 'No playing time tomorrow, we need your help.'

Avani bit her lip and said nothing. So that was that, she thought with a sigh. Going to Bhoot Byet was out!

***

The next day, when Ambar was returning from the field after helping his father gather fresh melons, he was hit by a stone. His thigh got badly bruised. He lost his balance and dropped the melons, spoiling most of them and earning the wrath of his father later. Ambar was quite sure someone had been lying in wait and had used a catapult to aim a stone at him. His father, though, was extremely displeased and did not believe him. 'Utter carelessness, Ambar. You will have to pick more melons. Make sure you do that tomorrow.'

No trip to Bhoot Byet for him either! By now the children were dying to go there.

Next, Tavishi got into trouble. She had just finished collecting four bundles of firewood, but then had to go to Avani's house to borrow some things. She kept the wood near the well on the edge of the long field. It would be safe there, she thought, there were never any robberies in Bagasra. Half an hour later, when she returned to take them home, there wasn't even a single bundle left! And no one had seen anyone take them. Her mother rebuked her sternly. 'Tavishi! Why have you become so careless? You should have done what I told you to, instead of going off. You are not go anywhere with your friends till the wedding is over.'

Tavishi was in tears. 'Avani, I collected so much firewood for the *chulah* outside, I spent so much time, and my mother thinks I'm not telling the truth ...'

Bhoot Byet was out for her as well.

Delshad, too, got into trouble for not bringing home the goats he had taken to graze. He kept saying, 'I did bring them back, someone let them out of the field ... they moved the goats away to the open field.' But no one believed him either.

All four of them had got into trouble! Avani's thoughts went round and round in a circle. 'I must think this through carefully,' she told herself.

In the coming days, mysterious things continued to happen. Two terracotta pots with beautiful designs on them, which had been kept especially for the wedding ceremony, were found smashed in Ketika's home. This was supposed to be an ill omen. No one knew how it had happened. Everyone shook their heads, but thought that a cat or dog must have knocked them over.

Why were these things happening? And why were toys found lying around after every incident? Was it the same person? Was someone getting them into trouble deliberately?

It couldn't be coincidence that all these things had happened only to the four of them and Ketika. How come something always happened so they could not go to Bhoot Byet? Why were only they constantly getting into trouble? Was someone preventing them from going to the island? And was that person also bent on spoiling Ketika's wedding? But who would believe Avani?

Was she being over-imaginative?

It was a mystery.

As Avani put clothes to dry on the hedges, she thought, Something doesn't seem right. It's scary and odd and I am frightened. But what can we do about it? I have no proof . . .

10

THE PRIEST KING ARRIVES

A whirlwind of activity started in the village. Ketika was getting married to the Priest King's son, and as the Priest King himself would be present, preparations were even more frenzied. Ketika's mother and he belonged to the same clan, and the marriage had been fixed many years ago by the family elders.

'You boys! Have you cleaned and polished the copper axes and the bone-handled knives with the sheaths? You know how we value them. Everything has to be spic and span for the Priest King's visit.'

'Ambar! Who has taken the goats for grazing?'

'Avani! Tavishi! Gather the flowers for boiling if you want a blue dupatta!'

'Who is going to collect the honey, berries and wild nuts?'

The entire village worked as one.

'Where is the cotton? It has to be spun!'

'Don't waste time, you girls . . .'

'Who will stitch the dried leaves into plates?'

Instructions, orders, laughter and fun . . . the most gaily-coloured clothes, the best gifts . . .

The men went hunting for wild boar and deer, whose meat would be cooked for the feast.

Ravit the potter was busy making bowls, plates and jars on his potter's wheel, with help from others.

There was feverish activity around, with each one doing something. Even the little ones helped in some way or the other.

Now the big question was, when would the Priest King arrive?

How were they to show their respect and regard for him? How should they welcome him? A house had been kept ready for him with bedding, food and water. The bathroom pipes and drains were in good working order, the well had a big copper jar tied to it to help in drawing out water. They had done all they could to ensure a comfortable stay for him and his many guests. These people were the elite of Mohenjo daro, who had gone to Lothal for a meeting and were to proceed to Kuntasi and Dholavira before returning to Mohenjo daro. They had matters of state importance to attend to. They had to show these city people how much hard work the villagers of Bagasra could do!

What would the Priest King be like? Would he be aloof or would he be the calm, regal person they had heard about? Would he wear his grand clothes all the time? What about his family? And which guests would he bring? Would he talk to all of the village people?

The villagers planned a grand welcome . . . as soon as they would get word of his arrival, they would greet him in a manner befitting such a high-ranking personage.

But a surprise was in store for them.

One evening, ten carts came carrying a few people—ordinary people, who entered the village without any noise or fanfare, and after making a few enquiries, went to Ketika's father's house.

This turned out to be the Priest King and his retinue! A Priest King who said, 'I have come to formally seek the hand of your daughter for my son in marriage. I come as a father, not as Priest King.' He and his companions were taken to the house kept for them, with a long, hall-like room where all preparations had been made for their stay. They were offered the best of Bagasran hospitality and soon, word spread about their arrival.

By evening, people had gathered to pay their respects. They were surprised to see that the Priest King was not wearing his famous gold headband with the unicorn and sacred inscriptions on it, nor the headdress with the horns.

The Priest King said, 'I am here as a father, to welcome my new daughter to my home. The morrow will bring some of my relatives from Dholavira. But one person among my companions is my honoured guest, and it is my humble request that he and his disciples be treated with respect. They came looking for me in Lothal, but I had already left, so they followed, and only last night did I meet this monk and his disciples.

'Meet a visitor who reveres our land, and then listen to his story. For Zhao Gao has come from China, the faraway country across the icy wind-tossed mountains, facing peril and often ill health, just to be with us.'

'Your Holiness, rest and eat, and all will be as you wish,' replied Ketika's father with humility and respect.

Later, the Priest King asked him to collect as many village people as he could.

'Let us all hear the story of the Chinese monk,' he said.

Everyone gathered, for this was a summons by the Priest King, however quietly and informally he had spoken. They had to obey this intriguing request!

The people of Bagasra settled down to hear the tale told by the wandering monk.

11

THE MONK'S STORY

'My story starts many, many years ago, where I was born, near the birthplace of the Yellow River in Tibet. This is high up in the Bayan Har Mountains, where the giant panda lives in the bamboo groves.

'I grew up working very hard—tilling the land, growing millet, helping with the chickens and pigs, and collecting herbs and roots, as my father knew various uses for them. I was very strong . . . in fact, I am still quite strong!

'One day, I received a message from the heavenly spirits that I had to become a monk. I began my study under the tutelage of a learned, all-seeing old monk, for which I was told to leave home. I was very young then.

'I went far away from my home, leaving behind a weeping mother, a proud father and many brothers and sisters, who waved me goodbye with fear in their hearts and tears in their eyes. But on everyone's lips were good wishes, and the blessings of our ancestors and our gods were with me.

'For many years I served and looked after my master,

the old monk, doing all the chores so that he was free for prayers. But I started getting restless. A sense of unease gripped me and I got a premonition of something momentous. I had strange dreams. I saw all the signs and symbols sent to me by my ancestors. I saw the moon, the stars, the sun, the rivers; I even dreamt of Pan Gu—yes, he who created the universe—and of Nu-wa, who repaired the sky, according to the legends. I saw the auspicious Sika or the White Plum Deer, a divine creature; also the lotus flower, a symbol of purity. During daytime, the legend of the birth of the universe was always with me. It was a strange time, of being awake, yet asleep; of sleeping, yet being wide awake.

'I thought of the great Emperor Huang Di, the Yellow Emperor from the Huang Ho or Yellow River. Later I actually met this revered monarch. His wife, Empress Xi Ling-shi, discovered how to make silk, and brought great wealth and fame to our country by cultivating the mulberry tree and rearing silkworms, and using their cocoons to get this prized silk, which is the biggest and best-kept secret of the Chinese world. States are ready to go to war for this secret.

'The elderly monk who taught me was wise and pious. He used to have visions, which would come true. When I told him my dreams, he said, "The time has come." He took me on a long journey, and we stopped at a village where the Yellow Emperor was to come.

'Oh, the ceremonies for his welcome! How elaborate they were! The preparations carried on for weeks—long bowers were made of bamboo plants, fir, cyprus, pine branches and conifers; a throne was made of old wood carved with smiling dragons, cranes and fish; plants, flowers, fruit and grain were offered; people brought the best they could. After all, their emperor, chief of the Five Tribes, was coming!

'I know not how my master managed it, but I was granted audience with the emperor. I was ignorant of what he had told my master earlier. I dared not question anything because I was under vows of silence. I only know that I was given a box with a secret compartment and instructed to keep it safe, and not tell a soul about it. I would know its use in some years; at the proper, auspicious time. My eyes were cast downwards. I was not permitted to ask any questions; my duty was total obedience to my master.

'So I kept it hidden and told not a soul.

'We came back and continued our prayers, meditation and penance.

'There came a day when I was on my own, as foretold. I bid goodbye to my master and teacher with great gratitude, reverence and much sadness. For some years I wandered, praying, keeping vows of silence and travelling, then teaching. Then I had a vivid dream. Again and again it was the same one, till I realized it was a vision and I had to act on it.

'I heard a voice tell me, "Go to the land across the mountains of your birth, go to Indeeya, Meluhha. For there will come to Meluhha many years from now a holy being, the Enlightened One. Go, and keep for him an offering which I shall describe to you. Ask for blessings for the ancestors of this land, for the ancestors of the emperor and for the future generations. Pray to your ancestor gods, use the green jade bi and the ts'ung. Beseech the gods to show you the way. You have to make this journey, this pilgrimage, to this far-off place through icy mountains and cold dry desert lands.

"But remember, always, you will be guided. For it is meant to be—you are the carrier, the instrument, bearing an offering to be kept in trust for the Enlightened One, many years from now, with the priest there. It could be fifty years, hundred years, one thousand years or two thousand . . . the gods count time in a different way from humans. You have to suffer, go through a harsh journey. Take this offering and give it. It will be difficult. You will often want to give up and return to your beloved land, but you must persevere and face all the difficulties with fortitude and courage. Then and only then will you know what to do next.

"Now open the lacquer box given by the Yellow Emperor Huang Di," continued the voice.

'I did so and found a small circular jade bi disc with a hole in the centre, which symbolizes the round heaven, and square ts'ung tubes, which signify the square earth. Jade is a precious stone of heaven and has mystical and spiritual significance, more important than gold or silver. Jade is used to venerate the earth deity too. It is given to priests who communicate with ancestor-spirits and gods. This was a great honour, but carried an even greater responsibility.

'Then I was told to look thoroughly, for there was something for my eyes alone. I looked even more carefully and pressed around. The base slipped! I had found the secret compartment. I was struck with wonder and amazement when I saw what lay there. For lo and behold, it contained a small length of fine, strong, light, shimmering silk—silk that was made in secret from the mulberry tree cocoons by the wife of the emperor.

'This beautiful piece of silk was to be taken as The Offering.

'I knew I had been entrusted with this holy task by the emperor. I was told to guard the silk, with my life if it so be, but never should it be allowed to fall into the hands of thieves and brigands, or unbelievers.

'So my disciples and I travelled through cruel deserts, frosty mountains, sunny valleys with serene blue lakes, and high beautiful grassy meadows called *jailoos*, full of butterflies and birds of jewel colours, and flowers of purple and pink, to come here.

'And this is my mission, to hand over this piece of silk in its box made with the sap of the lacquer tree. This has to be kept in a wooden temple, which has the Purification Pool, till the Enlightened One walks this earth.'

The monk went on to tell them about the bandit who had captured and then released them, which had ultimately resulted in their journey being made easier, of the help given by him and the reparation the bandit had made for hurting him.

Everyone listened with rapt attention to this fascinating narration. Nobody asked any questions. Zhao Gao's sincerity and earnestness could not be doubted. There was a ring of honesty in his voice.

Everything fell into place. This was a plan by the gods. It was a proclamation and it would come to pass.

That was the reason why the Priest King was here, in

this small village of Bagasra, with some powerful people, the elite of the great city of Mohenjo daro. This piece of silk from thousands of miles away had to be preserved carefully, with the utmost vigilance, for such a holy gift came but once in many thousand years.

The day of the wedding was decreed to be the auspicious day for handing over the silk to the Priest King at Gola Dhoro, amidst prayers for the holy prophecy to be fulfilled. Later in Mohenjo daro it would be formally placed inside the beautiful, polished lacquered box, and hidden away in a secret place in the wooden temple, known only to the Priest King and Zhao Gao. Only then would his holy mission be complete, and only then could the Chinese monk return to his far-off land of the Yellow River.

12

AROUND THE FIRE

The next day, as dusk descended and everyone finished their evening meal, they gathered outside, around the fire. Traditionally it was lit at night for safety, to ward off wild animals, but since the fields had been cultivated, that fear was less. It was time to relax and listen to grand tales of valour and bravery. There was singing and dancing. Tavishi's mother could sing beautifully, and so could Tavishi. Some people would act out scenes from stories. Dholaks and stringed instruments were played.

Today, however, was different. There were many guests who had come from near and far for the wedding to be held after two days. The whole village was geared to look after them, and friends from the nearby hamlets had been preparing visitors' meals and the grand wedding feast. In the evening they relaxed, happily tired after a long day of labour and preparation.

Ketika's father told them the story of the sacred necklace brought by the Priest King—the one with the green emeralds, blue sapphires and turquoises—from the far-off ravine of the Kokcha River. It would be adorned on Ketika by the Priest King's wife during the wedding ceremony.

The Elder said, 'This necklace is very powerful. The precious stones had been blessed by a holy rishi many, many years ago. It is said that whoever wears it will always have a priest in the family, a priest who will be king in a spiritual, religious way.'

The Priest King smiled gently and said, 'I knew good Bhoopat would tell this story, so I brought the necklace here. Amongst friends and family it can be safely shown, and I trust his people completely. Look at the necklace; see, it is an amulet too, protecting the wearer from bad luck and showering the blessings of the gods.'

The necklace was handed around. The ladies looked at it in awe and wonder. It seemed to glow and glint mysteriously in the flickering firelight. Yes, there was a strange power in those stones . . . in the green dazzle of the emeralds, in the flash of blue lightning from the sapphires . . . everyone could feel it. There were so many stories about this necklace. They all fell silent.

Ravit, Bholu, Sonu, Giri, Hiroo, Veeru—everyone held it, awestruck, and passed it around. Avani was handed the necklace as well, and child though she was, she, too, felt the solemnity of the moment.

Just then a baby started crying, and the stillness was shattered. Talking resumed.

Meanwhile the young groom, Keshav, was being teased and asked questions about all the rites he had had to go through to show the world he could protect and look after a wife and family.

He started telling them about the first night he had spent alone in the jungle—an ancient clan custom handed down from his ancestors.

'It was the first time I was alone, and I was very young and so scared! Every time I heard a rustle I thought it was a tiger or a fleet-footed leopard out to get me. I had to shoot a wild animal and bring it back as my trophy. I was terrified! But I did kill a wild boar—hid behind a tree and used my bow and arrows very effectively.'

Ketika called out, 'Oh, so I don't have to worry! No tigers will come and attack me!'

This caused much amusement around, as Ketika's aim with the bow and arrow was true and straight, and she could defeat most of the boys in Gola Dhoro in any archery contest.

Avani felt something brush near her hand; it was Manimaoo, the cat! He often trailed her without her knowledge and then brushed by her leg so she would realize he was there and talk to him! He licked her very rarely, only if she hadn't noticed him. The first time he'd licked her she'd squealed, 'Ooww! His tongue is so rough! Not at all like a dog's.' Now she stroked him gently and he seemed to like it.

It was getting late. Someone yawned loudly. Then one

by one, the children started nodding off to sleep. Time to leave. People started drifting off, talking about the next day.

'Tomorrow will be so much fun for us! The herb-leaf paste mixed with mehendi is ready, and we'll have a grand time,' the girls giggled as they put their heads together to play a practical joke on Ketika.

Next morning, all the ladies and the young girls gathered. They would get mehendi applied on their hands by the artistic Gatita. The mothers, busy finishing last-minute work on the wedding clothes, smiled at everyone's excitement as they stitched away, using bone or copper needles.

Gatita started the delicate mehendi drawing . . . the first one would be Ketika. There was dancing and singing, talking and laughing. Ketika's clothes were examined, and so was the jewellery given by her parents. Avani and Tavishi winked at each other.

At last everyone's mehendi dried.

'Ketika, let's see yours!'

'Rubada, keep still, I can't draw it if you keep squirming!'

'Tavishi, hey, that looks great!'

'Shiuli, the colour is so dark . . . she is going to be the next bride!'

'Sagari, what is that design?' Everyone burst out laughing, for Avani, who was NOT artistic, had tried to draw a peacock with lovely open tail-feathers, but it had ended up looking like a mango tree! Sagari had to wash her hands quickly, and Gatita drew a delicate swirling design instead.

'Hurry, girls,' called Ketika's mother.

Just then there was a loud yell, 'You bad girls . . . who did this?'

Naughty Avani and Tavishi had put two insects and one horrible yellow frog-like creature on top of the bundle containing Ketika's pretty clothes. The creature made an indignant sound and jumped off, even as Ketika leapt backwards! Ketika hated creepy-crawlies, as she called them. She was very brave when it came to wild boars and tigers . . . but put a lizard or a frog near her and the screeches would start!

Smothered chuckles and giggles gave the girls away and everyone laughed at Ketika, calling her a baby and various other friendly insults.

'We have a beautiful ceremony in a while,' said Avani's mother. 'Get ready for the evening, everyone!'

'I wonder what the groom's side will bring as gifts?' said eleven-year-old Sagari. 'Do you think we will get anything?'

'Don't be greedy,' her mother scolded.

'But Ma, all of you were talking about that last night. We heard you!' protested Sagari. 'Anandi Masi was laughing and saying that they come from far away, so they are bound to have different kinds of gifts for everyone.'

'Let that be, don't listen to grown-ups' talk!' her mother scolded, going pink.

The girls looked at each other and giggled . . . when their mothers had no answer ready, this was the usual reply they gave!

Truth be told, everyone was secretly wondering about the gifts. After all it was the Priest King's family, and he had travelled far. They had just come from Lothal, where ships from distant lands docked. The Fertile Crescent cities of Mesopotamia often sent various valuable articles made of gold there, which the wealthy merchants would buy in exchange for carved ivory articles. Maybe there would be pearls from Magan or Dilmun. Or maybe the Priest King would get a special seal for the family . . .

13

CEREMONIES

The main ceremony of the day was about to start. Just moments before, Avani's mother caught hold of her.

'Look at your hair—all that dancing and running around has made it a mess, and you have lost your hairpins! Come here. I'll have to comb it again. You look like a real jungle girl. Sit still while I untangle the knots.' She took out her lovely bronze comb and combed Avani's long, curly hair with vigour. When Avani's plaits were undone her hair usually became unruly. The ribbons or clips never stayed for any length of time with her.

Avani was suddenly pensive—she could feel a change was on the way, a sense of loss, but couldn't express it. Her father's saying flashed through her mind, 'For every beginning, someone pays with an ending.'

Everyone was dressed in their best. After all, weddings of this kind happened very rarely and had to be enjoyed to the fullest. Guests from the town of Gola Dhoro would also be there.

Soon there were many people in the long, open garden

fenced by thorny bushes. The Priest King himself was there, in his simple but stately attire. He wore a fine white-coloured dhoti and shawl with the regal three-leaf motif on the border. His right shoulder was bare. His hair was drawn back with a copper band, his beard neatly combed and he wore a headdress with ornaments over his ears. He looked serious, but kind and compassionate as well. Though not tall, his straight back gave him a stately look.

Keshav wore a dhoti and *angavastram*, with a simple necklace. His long hair was coiled and knotted.

The Chinese monk and his disciples were also among the crowd, but they just observed quietly, looking very interested. One of the disciples held a rolled scroll of cloth in his hands.

The ceremony started with five ladies carrying clay lamps, filled with sesame oil, placed on clay plates of a beautiful deep red colour, along with bowls of water, fruit, neem leaves, honey, curd, dates, salt, barley, wheat and fragrant flowers. The items on the plates glowed in the soft light of the lamps.

The largest plate had a beautiful painted border of black pipal leaves. Placed on it were green basil leaves, white jasmine and red hibiscus flowers. In the middle of it sat a statue of the Mother Goddess.

'Ma, is the Earth Mother ceremony beginning?' asked a child loudly.

'Shhh . . . yes, it has begun, now watch quietly,' his mother rebuked.

And the child watched, fascinated, as the ladies made the bride sit on a coloured straw mat. They circled her five times. Ketika had to eat the mixture of dates, curd, honey, bitter neem and salt, and she had to accept the other offerings of fruit and grain in her long saree pallav. Then together, they gave her the plate with the Mother Goddess figure. This was important, as the bride had to take it to her new home after marriage and ask for all favours first from this figure.

Ketika then had to pray to all the holy spirits, starting first with the fire and water spirits at the same time, so they were placed together. After that, everyone chanted prayers. Ketika's mother, wearing a saree and her gold necklace with round micro-beads, came with gifts, followed by the village people with their unique shell ornaments made especially for Ketika, and many other beautiful and useful presents. She was lucky that her journey to her new home would be by river boat, and she could carry all this with her!

As soon as the formal ceremony was over everyone wanted to see the gifts.

A jade ring! And a mottled jasper pendant to ward off dangers caused by waters! This was a most important stone, as all their villages were situated near waterbodies.

A bright turmeric-coloured saree! And a red carnelian bead necklace, with long, cylindrical and round beads, from their very own bead workshop! But what Avani and Tavishi loved the most was a bronze mirror, polished so thoroughly that the face was clearly visible.

'Ooo, I'd love that,' breathed Tavishi.

'You'll have to get married for that!' teased Avani, and everyone burst out laughing. Both girls loved pretty things, but Avani was always in too much of a hurry to look after anything well!

But what a surprise was in store for the villagers! First there were terracotta toys for all the children. Their eyes opened wide and there were sounds of happy laughter.

'Faience hedgehogs!' 'Steatite cubes!' 'Rams, parrots, hares, oxen carts!' Shouts echoed all around. For the adults there were prized gifts, which they got only rarely. There were also rudraksha malas for the whole clan. This was indeed special, as they had to be brought from the icy terrains of Nepaala, which had the highest snow peaks in the world. For the rudraksha tree grew only over there. They were indeed to be cherished; priceless and unexpected as gifts. The Priest King also gave the Chinese monks some rudraksha beads to take back.

Avani, in the meantime, went to help Ketika, who was sitting behind a fragrant curtain of white jasmine flowers. For the groom's side would now give her all the auspicious objects with which she would start her married life. Suddenly it struck Avani why she'd been feeling sad—she would miss Ketika, the fun they had had, their long talks. Change! But no time to think about that now . . .

There was anticipation in the air.

The groom's mother, wearing a bright saree, came forward with a large basket decorated with flowers and five conch shells. There were tiny pots of sweet perfumed oil and a length of wild silk and cotton, dyed red and yellow. There was jewellery—nose ring, earrings, bracelets, a copper waistband and a silver amulet with a three-headed feline to guard against misfortune.

The Priest King started with chants invoking the holy spirits. When the ceremony was finished, Zhao Gao cleared his throat. He said, 'I have watched your beautiful ceremonies where, very rightly and properly, you first invoke the gods and ancestor spirits for their blessings. Now I must give my blessings to the daughter of this house.'

He went to the young girl and Li Jinsong gave him the rolled-up cloth. Ketika received it in the traditional way. When it was opened the monk explained, 'This is a Chinese dragon that I have drawn for you. He is a kindly, wise dragon, a caring dragon, who does not breathe fire. See, he has five toes—that is very important! He is the guardian of the wind, the rain, the earth, fire, the rivers and precious metals, and will always look after you. And the crane I have drawn symbolizes good fortune and happiness. Always keep this, my child, and may both of you have great peace and prosperity.'

Slowly everyone started leaving. It was late and the

following day was the most important one—it was the day of the wedding!

Suddenly, there was an urgent call from one of the villagers, who was near the wooden temple.

'Look, someone has been inside, the sacred brazier has been thrown out . . . and the same toys are scattered around! Come fast!'

People went running. All the men—Akku, Babu, Ravit, Giri, Sonu and Hiroo—worked with a will and quickly cleaned the doorway and the altar area. Hirooda was the first one to take quick action and help clean the brazier, which was full of mud.

Who could have done this dastardly deed? Was this, too, going to be a bad omen for Ketika?

14

THE WEDDING

'Wake up, wake up, Avani, you have to collect flowers,' said her mother, shaking her awake.

Avani murmured sleepily, 'Later, Ma, later', and wrapped the warm shawl even closer, for early mornings were cool.

Then she sat up with a jerk. How could she be so stupid! What was she thinking of? Today was Ketika's wedding. So even though it was dark and cold, she had to get up. She would also get warm water for a bath today. Ooh, what a luxury!

She got ready quickly, bundling an old saree around herself. She would return later to wear her best clothes for the ceremony. Just then, Tavishi came to her house and together the two of them set out for the temple, where their other friends had also gathered. They had to pick flowers from the sacred grove behind the temple, which contained all kinds of flowers and shrubs and trees. It had a bael tree, with its holy leaves, the holy peepal tree and an akash neem tree as well. There were also trees bearing the

84

deep gold temple-flowers, and pink bell-flowers. Every kind of jasmine flower could be found: mogra, juhi, jai, chameli, all with their sweet fragrance, along with holy basil and other leaves the priests needed.

'Hurry!' called Tavishi, as she saw Avani sniffing the flowers. 'We have to be quick and pick the brightest flowers we can . . . the buds picked yesterday are already blooming in the garlands made by Pushpa Tai.'

The group then helped to decorate the low wooden temple. It had a wooden altar, and a metal brazier for burning wood and incense. The altar was decorated with fruit and flowers and grain. It held a figure of a holy man wearing a horned headdress, sitting cross-legged, with animals at his feet. He was called the Lord of Animals and the Lord of every living thing. The children quickly bowed, asking for blessings before starting the decorations. This was something that they had been taught when very young.

Across the ceiling, the flowers had been made into a beautiful canopy, so if you looked up it seemed like a sky full of blossoms. Directly below that was the clay container to hold the holy fire.

At the entrance was a copper jar of water. Most important, placed beside it were two copper knives with bone handles, and a small *parshu* or copper battle-axe to ward off evil spirits. There was a round carpet of holy leaves, flowers and lighted lamps in the centre, with space to walk on either side.

The bride and her parents entered to the sound of conch shells. Delshad and Ambar had the honour of blowing the shells. They blew as hard as they could, and the joyous, triumphant sound reverberated in the temple. Ketika looked beautiful in her turmeric yellow saree with a bright red pallav and loose blouse-like top. Her mother had put black kajal on Ketika's eyes and red-coloured paste on the lips, reminding Ketika how she had loved to dress up as a child. This lip-colour was famous in the land and was used by all the ladies. Ketika's long, dark hair was coiled in an elaborate style . . . how Avani and her friends had teased her while it was being done! She wore pretty orange shell clips and carved ivory combs on the sides of her hair. She also had on long gold earrings and a necklace. On seeing those the girls sighed . . . very few people got gold jewellery . . . how lucky!

The Priest King, his wife and the groom then entered in their regal outfits. Respects were paid to the departed souls of their families. It was a small, simple ceremony. Both sets of parents also participated in the various rites. A fire was lit in a clay bowl, and prayers were chanted. Avani held a round red clay jar of water, with a painted deer looking over his head at a tree, and mango leaves on the rim. Beside the holy fire were three tall red clay jars, also containing water.

The bride and groom had exchanged flower garlands, and were now praying to the sacred fire and all holy spirits for guidance and wisdom. After the prayers, Keshav's mother put the precious sapphire necklace around Ketika's neck, along with two bronze bangles on her arms, one of which had a humped bull drawn on it, the other an inscription.

Ketika's bronze anklets tinkled softly as she and Keshav walked, sat and again walked around the fire. Silver ear ornaments and a silver pendant and chain, brought from Mohenjo daro, were given to her. A wedding was a serious and sacred affair, and no one talked while the ceremony was on. When the conch shells sounded again, everyone showered the couple with barley grains, flower petals and leaves of holy basil. They were very careful not to step on the scattered grains, though!

The wedding was over. The couple had taken the blessings of all the elders and guests, asking them to partake of the blessed *prasadam*. There was only one important ceremony left, after the grand lunch.

The feast! This was what Avani, Tavishi, Delshad and Ambar had been waiting for!

'You, children, all of you . . . this side . . . sit down here,' they were told. They sat on straw mats spread on one side of the room. In front of each was placed a plate made of strong, thick leaves, along with two small bowls, also made of leaves.

Then the fun started . . . all the dishes reserved for special occasions were served. A mouth-watering pulao, delicious cakes made from fermented barley ground with herbs, date-and-wheat laddoos, honey-and-millet sheera—the array of dishes was vast and delicious. There were all sorts of fruits, different spicy meats and tangy-tasting fresh fish. The list was endless and seemed very grand, for the children were used to simple meals every day.

'Don't be greedy. We don't want you to get stomach ache,' one of the grown-ups called out to them. 'Or cavities! You'll need go to the teeth doctor and get your teeth drilled!'

The children simply grinned . . . they were having a grand time.

There was more food! Dried apricots, figs cooked in a curry, curd along with rotis . . . The ladies of Gola Dhoro had worked tirelessly, helped by women from the neighbouring hamlets, who had brought along delicious dishes as well. After all, today was special. A marriage, and the Priest King, his family and other officials as their guests . . . the village had gone out of its way to shower hospitality.

Zhao Gao and the two young monks were begged to eat well too, and enjoy the various types of food placed before them. Later, the monk had to go to the temple along with the Priest King, and hand over the silk cloth to him at the auspicious hour in the afternoon.

'Sir, it is an honour for us . . . your visit will be remembered for many generations,' said Ketika's father respectfully. 'Please partake well of our fare.'

Zhao Gao shook his head in amazement. In his land, only royals got to eat at this kind of feast. Peasants would never be able to do this! He had been told by the Priest King that the feast was as grand as any in Mohenjo daro.

'Your people seem so equal . . . there's not much difference between the rich and the poor, be it in houses, dresses or amusement,' he mused, as he sampled a little food.

15

AFTERWARDS

At the auspicious hour, Keshav and Ketika set out for the river for a simple ceremony of praying to the River Mother, facing the sun. The elders would follow. After that, they could do as they pleased. Only some small ceremonies were to be held at the Priest King's house after they returned to Mohenjo daro.

Soon Avani, the grown-ups and other children went to the river. It was a colourful procession, as everyone was still in their best clothes. The village dogs came along as well—anything for a run with friends! The path to the river was narrow and winding, with huge trees on either side and fields beyond. The parents had to thank all the elements. Ketika and Keshav received permission to leave and then set off home. The children frolicked happily, and the parents intoned the fixed, rhyming prayers required for the ceremony.

Then it was time to go back. There were still hours of daylight left, for the days were long and the nights short. The shaded path had many shrubs and wildflowers.

Suddenly, there was a commotion. A dog came running up, yelping and limping. There was a cacophony of noise as the other dogs joined in. An ox cart lost balance suddenly as the beast stumbled. A wheel broke and the cart overturned. After that, there was chaos. The dog kept running helter-skelter and finally some men caught and calmed it down. There were yells, shrieks, children running. Avani tried to quieten them. 'Ssh, ssh, it's nothing. No wild animal. Something just frightened the ox. It must have got a scorpion sting.

'Come on, stop crying, quiet, we'll leave, we'll leave . . . Baba, we are leaving.'

'Yes, yes, we are following too,' answered Ketika's mother.

The puzzled cart-driver said he thought a stone had hit the ox. It took a while for order to be restored, then they set off again. When they finally reached home they were all tired.

'Where are Ketika and Keshav?' Ketika's mother asked suddenly. 'They had gone ahead.'

'They aren't here,' said old Thatha, who kept a close watch on everyone's comings and goings. If he was awake, he knew everything.

Everyone started looking for them but they were nowhere to be found. There was a hue and cry . . . people ran hither and thither, shouting, calling, 'Keti! Keshav!' Where had they vanished?

'Missing, my Keti is missing,' wept her mother.

Five men went down to the riverside. The villagers ran to the Great Wall, to the north entrance gate of Gola Dhoro.

'Maybe they are at a shell workshop . . . Keshav was interested in seeing one,' said Ketika's father.

'But no one was working, they took time off today,' Avani's baba replied.

'I know he wanted to see the carnelian workshop, he told me so,' said Ambar.

Ravit the potter went to the Wall to check, but no one had seen the couple there.

Where were they? How did they disappear?

The remaining guests assembled. Some had already left for the hamlets, wanting to reach before dusk.

'Gather all the children,' a scared-looking lady suddenly said. 'We have to check that no one else is missing.'

'Come here, all of you! Bring the small ones too!'

Soon all the children had been accounted for, except one, little Manu. Where was he? Everybody started looking. Suddenly, Avani heard a whimper, and he was soon found, hiding under a bush.

'There he is, asleep. No, he's awake. Manu!' called his relieved father.

A scared, dirty Manu came out, rubbing his face. He clapped his hand to his mouth and looked frightened and bewildered.

'I have a message from a man . . . I don't know who he was; he had covered his face with a cloth. He looked scary.' The child shuddered, then continued, 'He said to me to tell you something important . . .'

'What are you talking about?' asked his puzzled father.

'About Ketika didi,' explained the child. 'See, here are her two copper bangles.

'Ketika didi and Keshav bhai are safe and they

want something,' he continued. Now everyone was listening intently.

'Some cloth,' he said finally, scratching his head.

'Cloth? I never heard such rubbish!' shouted his father as people started asking Manu what he meant.

'Let the child remember and tell us slowly,' added Avani's mother.

Manu stood looking at them, then said suddenly, 'The Chinese monk, they want his magic cloth. They also want the blue necklace. Put them in a box in the channa field, under the neem tree. And then they will send back Ketaki didi and Keshav bhai, safe and happy.'

No one could understand. They? Who were they?

'One more man, but I didn't see him. I heard him shouting, though,' Manu replied on being asked this.

'He said he would send them to you,' the child again repeated.

'My daughter! Oh Mother, goddess of all creatures, help us . . . where is she?' Ketika's mother sobbed, looking at the bangles and holding her head in her hands. The other ladies surrounded her, to calm her and offer hope.

'We have to think,' said Avani's father. 'What does this mean?'

Slowly they managed to figure out Manu's message.

Ketika and Keshav had been kidnapped! In exchange for their release, the kidnappers wanted the holy silk cloth, which the Chinese monk had given to the Priest King for safekeeping earlier in the afternoon. They also wanted the special family heirloom necklace, which had been given to Ketika . . . and which she was already wearing!

The men looked at each other silently, aghast. This was extraordinary. A kidnapping! Consternation was on every face. Demands made of the Priest King himself! Unheard of in peaceful Meluhha, a land of plenty, where there were hardly any bandits and thieves.

Now there was turmoil and fear in the air. Gola Dhoro had become a dangerous place. The Priest King's daughter-in-law had been kidnapped and the kidnappers' demands were frightening and unreasonable. The honour of the Priest King, the honour of their land, was at stake. It seemed they had blackmailers and robbers in their district.

'We will have to call the Priest King. Right now he is deeply immersed in his meditation,' said Manu's father, looking scared and troubled.

They were fearful of what the Priest King might say and do. Honour was very important to all of them, and their village, Ketika's safety and the honour of the Priest King were now all linked.

'Who will tell him?' asked Bhoopat, Ketika's father, his terrified voice breaking into the unnatural quiet. He had just returned, running swiftly back from the riverside.

'My daughter . . . let her be safe . . .' he kept murmuring. 'What will he say, a kidnapping here and that too, members of his family!'

A collective shudder of anger and fear seemed to pass over them.

Action! That was what was now required.

16

SEARCH

Who had taken away Ketika and Keshav?

Manu had to be questioned slowly and gently.

'Start at the beginning, child,' Ketika's father said. 'Where were you? Who talked to you?'

The child wrinkled his brow, looked at them and said slowly, trying to remember, 'He said, "Tell them Ketika is safe. Bring the silk cloth here before sundown. Put it in a box in the channa field, under the neem tree, then Ketika didi will come home. Otherwise things will be bad for the Priest King's family."'

A murmur arose, increasing in sound.

Avani gave an anguished cry, 'And I was supposed to look after Ketikadi! I am going to find her.'

No one paid any attention to Avani. She sprang up, and Tavishi, Ambar and Delshad followed her.

The men talked for a few minutes and formed a plan of action. Bhoopat, the Village Elder, took charge.

'Ravit, Veni and Giri, go search the riverside. You others, go back inside the town and search,' he ordered. 'Even the locked workshops. These people seemed to know where to go; they have planned this so well. They even knew exactly when to go to the river.'

'What about the small jungle?' Avani's baba asked. 'The trees are quite dense, though it is not so big.'

'Yes, someone must go there,' said Bhoopat in a decisive voice.

Some men ran inside Gola Dhoro, but no one there had seen Ketika or Keshav. They searched the mud-brick houses and looked into the adjoining workshops, but no luck. They searched the storerooms, where there were sacks of goods, kept for transporting to other cities. They looked for signs of a struggle or bits of clothes or bangles, but could not find anything. They checked the small granary, inside courtyards, near wells, but saw not a sign.

Near the river, the men fanned out. No boat was visible; still, they decided to paddle along the river banks and visit the next village.

The children were supposed to be at home, though no one had specifically told them so.

'Avani, don't get in anyone's way now, this is not the time,' her mother had cautioned. 'Don't bother anyone with questions. Now go away.'

So they had slipped away, and had decided to go search near the thick wooded area everyone called the jungle, although it had no tigers or lions. Along the way Tavishi tripped, and Avani stopped to help her. The boys ran ahead, but then they too paused in their tracks. Small sounds, muffled human noises could be heard. To the left, deeper inside! They raced on till the sounds were louder. No animal would be around with the noise they were making! It was darker and denser inside the woods now. They desperately hoped that they would find Keshav and Ketika somewhere.

Thank the heavenly skies! There was Keshav, tied tight to a tree! He had a huge bump on his head, with a bad wound; one leg was injured and bleeding copiously, his face was dirty and clothes dishevelled. His wedding earrings and chain were missing, his lips cut and swollen. The boys untied him and helped him on to his feet. Avani and Tavishi also caught up with Ambar and Delshad in the meantime. They shouted with relief when they saw Keshav.

'Exactly what happened? Where is Ketikadi?' they all asked, looking at a furious Keshav. Between agonized gasps and ragged breaths, Keshav's laboured words slowly helped piece together the story.

'They took her away! What cowards they were!' Keshav exclaimed. 'They came from behind, so softly, and pulled my hair. I stumbled, then I was caught, my hands held in a vice-like grip. A cloth was thrown over my face.

'I heard Ketika yelling and struggling. I twisted, somehow freed my hands, pulling the cloth off. Then I was knocked out with a stick! When I came to I heard Ketika yelling. I saw her kick, hitting the man, till he pinned her on the ground. She had even bitten his hand.

'They told me not to fight them, else they would harm her. They wanted the holy silk cloth. And they laughed evilly, saying that Ketika had the other thing they wanted . . . our holy family necklace, which she was wearing! They threatened me, telling me that my respected father had to give the Chinese cloth, or our honour and that of our land would be in jeopardy.

'I was blindfolded, hit again, tied to the tree . . . then they left me. I saw Ketika throw a rock at one of them . . .'

The children listened silently, after which the boys half-carried him till they came across some of the villagers. Keshav narrated his story to them again, after which he said, 'They said they would ask for the cloth to be kept in a big box under the large neem tree in the long field, near the eastern gate. It would be collected at 6 p.m., and no one should be there at the time.'

The villagers patted the boys and took Keshav back with them.

Soon the drums would sound, and the neighbouring villages would come to help. Someone would go to Kuntasi; a cart would set out for Rangpur. Yes, this search would involve everyone in the Harappan lands.

17

CLUES

After the men had left with Keshav, Avani said determinedly, 'Let's think of all the secret places that the men may have taken Ketikadi to. Then we'll pair up and go in different directions. We have to find her. I was supposed to look after her . . . I feel so bad . . .' Tears filled her eyes.

'Oh, don't be so silly,' interrupted Tavishi gently. 'That was just for the wedding . . . not afterwards.'

Looking serious, Ambar asked, 'If we had to hide, where would we go?'

'Upriver?' wondered Delshad. He had a sinking feeling that he and Ambar would be told to go there. They should all go together, but that would not be sensible.

Whenever anything important happened, Avani naturally became the leader. They looked up to her. She was fair, intelligent and always ready to take on the tough, dangerous tasks.

'Maybe they left for Dholavira, on Khadir Byet. They

could leave Meluhaa by boat . . . go to some far-off land,' said Ambar.

Everyone looked horrified.

'Oh, poor Ketididi!' Tavishi said with a catch in her voice. 'They won't harm her, I hope? Oh, why didn't she give them the necklace! Maybe then they would have left her alone.'

Avani said scornfully, 'As though Ketikadi would do that! It's the honour of her new family—no, no, she would have fought hard. She must have missed having something handy, like a stout stick, to defend herself.'

They fell silent.

Then Avani jumped to her feet.

'Look, we aren't helping anyone or anything by just sitting and discussing it,' she said. 'Let's go in two different directions; maybe we'll see something the grown-ups have missed.'

Tavishi agreed a bit timidly.

'Tavi and I will go downstream,' said Avani decisively. 'You boys, go to the big soap nut tree. Check carefully for any ring or earring or cloth or even threads on the ground . . . anything that proves that Ketikadi had been there.'

Ambar looked rebellious—he wanted more action than checking the stupid field near the soap nut tree. But he and Delshad had found Keshav after all! The boys set off towards the field while the girls walked towards the river. Not a soul was there; it had been thoroughly searched by the village men.

Tavishi and Avani looked carefully, but no rings, bangles or pieces of saree-cloth were to be found. The short, sharp shadows of the early afternoon had given way to longer, more ominous shapes. Each child secretly believed that they'd find something. They continued walking, wondering, would Ketika ever be found?

'So many jasmine flowers—the ladies have been careless,' Avani remarked idly. 'They are strewn all over the path—couldn't have knotted the garlands properly.'

Then she stood still. 'By the blue skies! What did I just say, Tavi? Repeat what I said.'

Obediently Tavishi repeated it. To her surprise, Avani started jumping and leaping with joy. 'Hey! I said it. What a fool I am! How stupid could I be?'

Tavishi looked at her uncomprehendingly.

'Look, Ketika has been very clever—she must have been so desperate and yet she thought of this! See, she's left some kind of trail with the flowers. We just have to follow it!'

Avani felt relieved and excited. They might be on the right path, at least now there was something to do . . .

'We have to follow this! Come fast.' Avani bent down once more, and pursued the flower trail like a dog. Both looked for jasmines and the special green leaves entwined in the garland. Now that they knew what they had to look for, they were very thorough. Along with them came Manimaoo the cat, walking regally but lightly. The flowers had been thrown randomly, so that sometimes the trail ended near a thorny bush, and at other times the path was completely devoid of even a single petal. Whenever that happened Avani would get anxious and exclaim, 'We've lost her! Please, please Mother Earth, help us, please, please . . .'

All the time the river flowed by placidly, often unseen, but the girls knew every curve it took, everywhere it went.

'Do you realize, Avani, that we've never left the riverside? We return to it after a couple of turns each time. They must be making sure no one saw them, that's why they took this roundabout route,' commented Tavishi.

Slowly, they realized that the trail had ended . . . no more flowers, no other clues. There was no sound or sign of anyone having passed from there. They sat down under an old neem tree, wondering where to go next. The trail was cold . . .

Manimaoo came and pressed himself against Avani's knee, then went forward, looking back and stopping, as if to say, 'Get a move on, don't dawdle.'

'We are, you know,' Avani told Tavishi.

'What? Don't know what you mean,' replied Tavishi.

'We are dawdling. Let's think where we should go.'

They crossed a small, bare patch which had only ber berry bushes, some already red. Walking fast, looking left and right, they noticed more ber than usual lying on the ground.

'Looks like Ketika has now used ber for her trail,' Avani said.

'Look at where your silly cat is sitting. Is he planning to come with us or not?' said Tavishi, a little irritated. 'Come on Manimaoo . . . oh, oh, look what is caught in his claws!'

Next she gave a shout. 'It's a ball of yellow thread, maybe from Ketika's saree. There is some on the bush too, right at the bottom!'

'Thanks be that Manimaoo was there, we'd have missed

it otherwise. Lucky it got caught in his paw,' Avani said as she stroked him.

She looked up sharply as a thought struck her.

'Tavishi, aren't we near the old ghat, where Baba's old raft is? No one goes there now . . . Tavishi, Tavishi, what if they have taken Ketika to Bhoot Byet?'

18

TRACK AND TRACE

Once that idea had got into the girls' heads, nothing would get rid of it.

'If we tell the grown-ups, they won't believe us and will order us to stay out of it. Let's just go. We'll take a raft,' said Avani, her voice shaking with both fear and excitement.

This time, very sensibly, they searched for a tough-looking raft.

'No,' Avani suddenly decided. 'Let's look for a boat. It's faster and safer. Together we paddle well.'

They did manage to find a sturdy boat and set off immediately. Manimaoo jumped in as well, making the boat sway.

Paddling hard, both went further downstream. They could see another boat far ahead—probably someone searching for Ketika. It was slowly becoming a speck in the distance.

As soon as their boat reached a calm stretch of water, the girls crossed to the other bank.

Tavishi, looking very serious, said, 'You know, I have

this feeling you are right. No grown-up would ever think of Bhoot Byet; and why would anyone go there? No one has gone there for years and years.'

'Yes, maybe one of those men will then go to Gola Dhoro and hide, and the other will wait and watch—Keshav did say that someone would watch,' remembered Avani.

Tavishi added, 'He would take the cloth and give it to his friend, and only then would Ketika be brought back.'

Avani exclaimed, 'What if they take the cloth and don't return Ketika! Oh holy spirits, protect her! We are close by, and with so many people searching, if Ketika is around, she will be found—and if we go to Bhoot Byet, at least we'll have checked whether she is there.'

Tavishi now started paddling while Avani rested. After rescuing Avani, she'd practised hard and become a strong paddler now.

'Wonder what the boys have found?'

'Little do they know how clever Ketika has been!'

As they neared Bhoot Byet, both girls fell silent. After their last two visits they easily recognized the long arm, the jutting-out tree and the rocks at the side. Rowing alongside the rocks near the tree, close to some bulrushes, they moored the boat at a suitable spot. They jumped out and ran, Manimaoo stepping delicately from rock to rock. Both of them felt scared—if the men were here, there would be great danger! Avani kept thinking of how they'd get Ketika home. Three young girls against cruel and dangerous men . . . her mind raced with possible ways and means to outwit them.

They looked around cautiously. No sign or sound of people. The island was calm and quiet in the early evening sunshine. Nothing bad or violent could happen here, could it? wondered Avani.

Both girls hitched up their colourful sarees to prevent them getting caught on some brambles or dry grass. They decided to go to the pit where Ambar and Delshad had fallen. The half-built brick walls of the huts couldn't hide anyone.

'Let's keep to the green patches, so we won't make much noise,' whispered Avani. Taking quick, terrified looks around, slowly and steadily, they went forward. Every rustle, every tiny flutter had their hearts hammering. Manimaoo was the best . . . he just vanished!

They neared the pit. No noise, only an eerie silence. Avani felt the hairs on her scalp prick. In spite of the sun and the bright flowers, there was an air of unease, almost of menace.

What would they find?

They soon knew.

Nothing.

The pit was as they had left it, filled with piles of leaves, some mouldy, some dry . . . that was all.

Avani was bitterly disappointed. She had imagined a scene where they would find Ketika in the pit, tied to a rock, and rescue her with cleverness and cunning.

Where should they look now? Surely the kidnappers wouldn't leave Ketika alone tied to a tree as well? Had all that quick paddling and coming to the island been in vain?

The girls sat on a log of wood, which seemed to be hidden away, tucked under some trees, disappointed and downcast.

'Mother Earth! Help us! Help us,' both prayed silently.

'I have been named Avani after you, oh Earth! Please show us the way,' Avani begged.

Tavishi was also sending up similar silent prayers, 'Mother Earth, my name symbolizes courage, I am the riverbed, I am named after you. Send some sign . . .'

Suddenly Avani got up, looking determined.

She was not going to give up.

'Tavishi, we haven't looked everywhere,' she said. 'We can't give up like this. I have this strange feeling she is here. Let's start again.

'The caves! We forgot the caves! We never did come again. Let's go, quietly now,' she whispered.

Wish we could have found something of Ketika's, at least we'd know if are on the right track, Avani thought.

They walked till they saw the hillock, half-hidden by trees.

'Now we'll be very careful, no talking,' she whispered.

They still looked down every few steps, then up, raking the bushes with sharp glances. Maybe they'd find some sign that Ketika was there.

Suddenly Tavishi clutched hold of Avani and stood transfixed.

'Look, look . . .' she whispered. At her feet lay a peach-coloured shell clip—Ketika's clip! It had to be hers. Both Avani and Tavishi wore ordinary white shell clips because Avani, especially, was careless and either broke or lost them in her haste. Her mother said it was no use giving her delicate things!

Ketika's clip! That meant Ketika was there! Both made a sign of victory. They had tracked her!

19

GIRLS TO THE RESCUE

As they crept, Avani's heart was thudding and Tavishi was petrified. The thugs were certainly there; they had proof, so this was no longer a guessing game, this was reality. Only the thought that Ketika was at the mercy of these evil men made them continue.

The girls were now close to the hillock, crawling almost at snail's pace, but where were the caves? Why hadn't they visited Bhoot Byet again? Not having explored it fully was a real disadvantage now. Hoping for some sound to guide them, they proceeded. Avani knew she should have some plan of action ready for when they would find Ketika. She pulled Tavishi back, and they retraced their footsteps till she thought it was safe to whisper.

'How do we rescue her if the men are guarding her?' Tavishi asked.

'We didn't see another boat, so maybe one of them took the boat back,' Avani replied. 'There will be only one man left here. We'll have to outwit him.'

'Maybe their boat is well hidden, like ours is, behind

some rocks or bulrushes, and we didn't notice it,' said Tavishi.

Avani thought for a while.

'I have to somehow take Ketika's place and the two of you should return to the village,' she said. 'The other man must have gone back to collect the sacred silk cloth—he knows the Priest King will not let Ketika be kept hostage till after nightfall. So he will definitely return, but we have enough time.'

Tavishi nodded. The plan made sense.

They reached the hillock without hearing any noise, although they'd expected yelling or crying. But there was just the twittering of birds and the occasional rustle of a small creature in the grass. It was eerily quiet. The opening of the cave seemed small, and very dark.

What had appeared a dark cave from a distance turned out to be a big boulder. With great trepidation, they went forward, Avani in the lead. Close to the rock was a cavity—a small, low opening. Again, no sound could be heard. They crouched. Avani put her head inside. There was no place to stand so she tried to crawl in and was out in a second, shaking her head.

It was just an opening . . . not a cave! She'd been overpowered by the strong animal odour they knew so well. It smelt of rats, rotten straw, bats, damp and old nests—it had huge spider cobwebs, swathes of which hit her face and when she reached up, her hands touched them. A whiff was enough to tell her no one was inside. With great presence of mind she managed to avoid screaming, but was out in double quick time.

No luck! Where could Ketika be?

'Let's just walk slowly round this hillock,' Tavishi suggested.

On the other side of the hillock, a strange sight met their eyes. Near some bushes was a wooded copse. From one of the trees hung a thick rope, knotted at intervals, tied to a stout branch. Avani's eyes popped out. The rope was doubled up, but dangling. She ran towards it, then stopped dead in her tracks.

A few feet away was another pit, obviously freshly cleaned, covered with new branches. A finger on her lips, she moved forward while Tavishi kept guard, as the same thought struck them both . . . Ketika was imprisoned there.

Lying on her stomach, Avani inched closer. She reached the rim of the pit and gasped. It was quite deep, and the light was not good, but she could see Ketika sitting on the rough ground! Ketika's hands were tied, a big scarf was wound around her mouth and tied tight. She was alone . . . no guard!

Avani called out softly to her, signalling to Tavishi to let her know she should let the rope down. Sure enough, in a trice, the rope was near her. The pit was not very deep, but anyone inside could not get out easily.

In a few seconds Avani was inside, sliding down the rope, glad of the knots, which prevented her from slipping down and hurting herself. Tavishi was turning her head in all directions, darting sharp glances right and left—was the enemy around?

In a flash Avani had pulled off Ketika's gag, untied her hands, given her a hug of relief and whispered the plan.

'Ketikadi, we'll exchange sarees. How come you have covered your head? I'll do the same,' Avani said softly.

They exchanged clothes even as Ketika demurred. She wanted Avani to escape with them too.

'No,' said Avani. 'When the kidnappers come here and see me they won't suspect anything. It will give you both a head start, till they find out that I am not you. I don't think they will notice at once. Now come, quickly tie the scarf around my mouth and tie my hands as well.'

'But what's this, where is your necklace? Have they taken it from you?' she continued, her eyes wide with apprehension.

'No,' replied Ketika. 'You know what I did when he asked for it? I gave the kidnapper an ordinary necklace, made of lapis lazuli! The one my mother got at the haat. And he doesn't know that!'

In spite of the danger present around them, the three girls giggled triumphantly.

Ketika continued, 'The other one addressed him as Anoush; that much I heard. But they kept their faces covered, so I couldn't really see them. Anoush had a red beard and wore a dirty green turban, that's all I could see.

'I told Anoush right there in Bagasra that since I was married I would cover my head, and he agreed. I've hidden the actual necklace in the knot in the waistband of my saree . . . I heard them saying that they had first only wanted the necklace, then heard of the cloth too. It would give them power, they believed.'

Ketika tied Avani's hands, but with one hand lower, the rope looser and a weak knot, so that Avani could undo it. She tied the cloth over Avani's mouth exactly the way hers had been tied, and, using the rope, was out of the pit at once. There was no time to lose. Then Ketika pulled up the rope to throw it, but suddenly changed her mind. She went down again and untied the gag and the rope which bound Avani's hands, ignoring Avani's urgent protests.

'No, Avani,' she muttered sternly. 'You must listen . . . we'll be three against these two, we can do something. They may overpower you and impose the same conditions for your release . . . hurry, hurry.'

Avani had no choice, so turn by turn they went up.

Tavishi quickly threw up the rope the way it had been, making sure it was securely over a branch, and the three raced to the river shore.

'We'll have to hurry,' Ketika gasped. 'That other man has gone to get water from a well, and to check if Anoush is on his way back.'

The three hastily moved away from there and, going round the hillock, started back in total silence. As they silently ran down to the water's edge, they wondered if they'd run into the other mysterious kidnapper.

20

ESCAPE!

Nearing the boat, Tavishi saw a stork rising clumsily in the air, screeching. She froze with fear. She clutched Ketika's arm, saying urgently, 'See that stork . . . he has been disturbed . . . maybe the man knows you have escaped and is coming here!'

Avani spoke urgently, 'Quick, Tavishi, Ketika . . . we have to hurry . . . Manimaoo, Manimaoo, come quickly!'

Ketika was rubbing her hands, which were sore and cut after being tied so tightly.

They did not see any other boat. As they were pushing their boat out they heard a huge bellow. Then there were baffled shouts of, 'Who's there? Who are you? Come back! You . . . you . . .'

Avani gave a start. That voice! That gruff clearing of the throat! The same man, near the tree! Had it also been him on the day of the fire? He was wearing a long brown turban, with his face covered by its end. She concentrated on the boat, as the man was just a few feet away from them. The girls' fingers had become clumsy with fear, but they hurried.

Avani was silent as she took the oars. Ketika's hands were still numb, and she felt as if she had pins and needles in them.

They had started moving when they heard his loud, enraged yelling.

'Stop! Who are you?! Wait till I catch you! Ketika! Stop! Or you will be sorry when I catch you!'

As the man was about to jump from a small rock to a larger one they saw an amazing sight. Out of nowhere Manimaoo leapt on him! He lost his balance, and as he struggled up, Manimaoo snarled viciously, and gave a hissing, screaming meow. Then the cat extended its sharp, deadly claws and drew them across the man's forehead, and when he yelped in pain, moving his hand to instinctively cover his eyes, it scratched his neck. He tried to fling Manimoo off, but he clung to the kidnapper's dhoti, and raked his claws along his calf.

As the man bent down to pull Manimaoo off, feeling terrified of this sudden fury from hell which had descended on him, he slipped on the rock and fell. His head hit another small rock, and he lay still, face down. He had been knocked out, and that too because of Manimaoo!

The three petrified girls wanted to cheer. They saw the cat jump from rock to rock, run along, till it reached a point from where it took a flying leap from a boulder and landed in the boat!

They were safe. But they knew they had to paddle faster, as the man would certainly swim out to the boat as soon as he became conscious. The infuriated shouts of the 'villain' before Manimaoo attacked him still rang in Avani's ears.

Of course, Manimaoo was the hero of the hour, but he ignored everyone and cleaned himself most assiduously.

Avani laughed in joy and relief, saying, 'Tavishi, now none of you can tease me about the cat who walks alone . . . it's because of Manimaoo that we are safe!'

Ketika glanced at her sore wrists, however, this was the least of her worries. Of them all, she realized the most how important it was to reach home safe and sound.

Then Ketika explained something which had been bothering Avani till now.

'Avani, remember the toys you found? It was this man who did all those horrid things you told me about. Every time he would leave behind a few toys, just to confuse everyone. The bizarre robberies, with the little ones crying and insisting they hadn't lost the toys, and no one believing them . . . He thought he was so clever, he boasted a lot about that.

'They were the ones who purposely broke the lovely red pots in my home, they locked Avani in the shed, stole Tavishi's firewood to get her into trouble . . .'

'But why?' asked Avani, surprised. 'Why would they want us children to get into trouble?'

'To prevent any of you from going to Bhoot Byet again,' explained Ketika. 'They visited the island after overhearing you talk about your visit there, and cleaned up another pit, and made it ready for me. Yes, one of them even used a catapult and aimed a stone at Ambar. I still don't know who they are ... they kept their faces covered. They did all the mean things to trouble us ...'

'And those acts were so childish that no one would suspect a grown-up of doing things like that. You'd think a man would break a raft, or something. And our people thought all these were stupid, childish pranks ...' Avani's voice trailed away. The riddle of the toys was solved, and it was just as she had thought.

As they reached the old ghat, Avani again adjusted her saree-pallav. It was more difficult than she had imagined, on the river, because it would keep flying up and flapping on her face. She had to pin it down with Tavishi's ivory clips, and just hoped they wouldn't break!

Walking by the riverside, they could hear faint sounds of people talking. For one frightening moment they thought it was the kidnapper! Then they heaved a collective sigh of relief ... no, he could not catch up with them ... he had no raft or boat to get there. They were safe!

The boat was made fast, and they jumped off, Manimaoo being the first.

The shadows were long and slanting now. They walked hurriedly for five minutes when out of the blue, Avani felt a rough hand close over her mouth.

'You thought you were so clever, didn't you? But I've got you now!' a voice hissed savagely in her ear.

Ketika and Tavishi both turned and saw a red-bearded man wearing a dirty green turban shoving and dragging Avani as fast as he could. They ran to attack him, kicking him, pulling him away from Avani as he pushed her along. Avani resisted as best as she could, but he was stronger. Another nightmare ... no, no, no, she almost cried, not

after all they had done to get Ketika out! *Go, go Ketika, run while you have time, that's more important*, she screamed in her head as she tried, futilely, to push his hand away. He was now using his feet, kicking out at the two girls.

By fluke, Avani managed to hit the man's stomach. He yelled in pain and his grip loosened. Avani twisted out of his grasp and managed to run, while Ketika and Tavishi attacked him again. He used brute strength to push them down and ran after Avani, shouting, 'You won't escape me this time!'

With a bound he caught up with her, picked her up and continued running, though slowly, as Avani was no docile captive. She pulled his hair and beard, and heard him curse. He was gasping, his breath coming in painful bursts. Stumbling, he continued till he reached the old ghat. That was his undoing.

For help was at hand for the girls!

Voices were heard, which materialized into people . . . their people! They came running, caught hold of the man and freed Avani from his tight grasp.

Of course, he had mistaken Avani for Ketika, because she was wearing Ketika's wedding saree and had covered her head!

To the man's chagrin the villagers managed to overpower him, while he gnashed his teeth helplessly, and swore roundly. Very soon his hands were tied, and he was their prisoner, guarded by four tough men.

What relief and rejoicing there was! The three girls' fathers were there, as were Ambar and Delshad. Some villagers had noticed the boys in the field near the soap nut tree, and, much to their dismay, they had been forbidden to go anywhere.

Avani's father hugged her, with tremendous relief on his face. His daughter was safe! Tavishi's and Ketika's fathers echoed his feelings in heartfelt words.

'The girls are safe!' This news reached both mothers, who had been completely overwrought, thinking their daughters too had been kidnapped.

Everyone talked, asked questions, interrupted and had their say for the first five minutes. It was complete chaos. Ravit the potter had already given the glad tidings to the Priest King. Keshav and he would be there in a short while, then everyone would go to Ketika's house.

When he met them the Priest King hugged Ketika,

like any father would, profoundly thankful that she was unharmed. Everyone forgot he was the Priest King; they only witnessed his gratitude to all the holy spirits, for keeping her and Keshav from danger and hurt.

Keshav, too, was received with warmth. He was limping because of his injuries and looked pale, but he was overjoyed to see Ketika safe and sound.

21

KETIKA'S STORY

The whole party soon reached Ketika's home and sweet, hot, reviving drinks were brought for the three girls. Then everyone settled down to hear Ketika's story.

'As soon as Keshav was tied up, I was blazing with anger,' she began. 'I hit out at them, I kicked, I tried to bite. They threatened to injure Keshav badly, and I could see they were serious. I controlled my anger because I didn't want Keshav to be hit or tortured more. They called me a wildcat!

'They pulled me away from Keshav and made me walk on. I told them that as I was now married, they should not touch me. They agreed, I think because they were secretly afraid of the Priest King's power and authority.

'I said I wouldn't run away or scream, but they took no chances. They gagged me. I pulled my saree-pallav over my head and covered most of my head and face, to which they didn't object.

'See, I had this idea that I'd try and leave some kind of trail, hoping people would notice. Luckily, before I had gone to the river, I'd been grumbling about the heavy weight of my hairdo, so my mother had combed it out and just made a normal long plait, and put flowers . . . yes, pinned jasmine strings with orange shell clips. So I pretended to hurt my foot, just to gain time. I had pulled my plait in front when they gagged me and soon, I started pulling out the flowers and scattering them as I went. I walked slowly because of my "hurt" foot. The men were getting impatient but couldn't do anything. One gave me a baleful look and said of course my foot would hurt, I kicked like a wild ass!

'Then those evil men went in the opposite direction to where we were headed and purposely threw my copper anklets, my rings and bangles here and there to create a false trail. I heard them boasting about their cleverness.'

'Yes, yes,' shouted Tavishi's father, while others nodded their heads in agreement. 'We found so many of her things . . . including a bronze mirror.'

'But my bronze mirror is at home . . .' said a puzzled Ketika.

'Then it's not yours. They just used someone else's to trick us into thinking that you had been taken from that side. There was nothing for quite a distance, then another anklet just like yours, and a ring, conveniently stuck on a bush at eye level, and such a long way too, so we thought maybe you had somehow managed to put it there,' explained Avani's father.

'Oh, I know!' exclaimed Avani. 'I had seen these two men earlier, the day all of you had gone to the grand haat . . . remember, I was punished so I was here in the village looking after the children? We were playing hide-and-seek and I saw them.' She repeated the conversation she had overheard, the things she had seen and how nothing had made sense. Delshad and Ambar supported her vociferously—Avani had told them all about it when they had returned from the haat!

'So they wanted to see how her things looked . . . they must have been planning this kidnapping for so long! And they didn't want anyone to wonder why Ketika's things were missing, or put her family on their guard, so they returned them,' concluded Avani.

Ketika continued her story, though by now everyone had practically guessed the details.

'I had already taken off the special sapphire, emerald and turquoise necklace, pretending I was retying my saree while hobbling along! I managed to put it in my waistband-knot, my pallav covering everything. With so many other necklaces on my neck, no one missed the special necklace. I hoped with all my heart that someone would realize I had left a trail, and that the jasmines were not just random flowers . . . thank the holy skies for Avani and Tavishi!'

'So if you were walking with them, how did you manage to leave that trail of flowers?' asked someone—by now everyone knew how Avani had tracked her down.

Ketika continued, 'Oh, the rude one walked ahead, to check if anyone was around, and the other, Anoush the red-bearded one, and I walked behind. He was carefully checking if anyone was following, or if anyone had realized that the trail they had left was a false one! So he didn't pay much attention to me, as long as I continued walking, and I had formed this plan . . . a little far-fetched, but I had to try something!

'The rest you know—I was taken to the island, put into the pit . . . it was scary, but they didn't bother me, except to tie me up. Then Anoush left, taking the boat, I imagine. After that I stayed in the pit till Avani and Tavishi came to the island . . . '

The ordeal was over! The grown-ups would make everything safe now.

The village people had, in the meantime, laid plans to set a trap to catch the kidnapper. They had thought of secretly watching the place selected for depositing the silk cloth. Next, they would trail him from there. That was no longer required, thanks to the girls! Instead they had to send a boat to Bhoot Byet and catch the other kidnapper.

Now that the girls were safe, many questions had to be answered.

How did they know about Bhoot Byet? When did they first go there? Why there and nowhere else? They finished answering all the questions and yet the excitement continued.

Zhao Gao, Li Jinsong and Wu Shaozu had listened avidly to every word. Zhao Gao shook his head, saying sorrowfully to the Priest King, 'All this because of the offering I brought! I feel sorry that you were made to suffer so much.' And he shook his head again.

22

CULPRITS UNMASKED

Suddenly there was the sound of running steps and thumping noises. A guard burst into the gathering, then stopped. He bowed to the Priest King, saying formally, 'Forgive me for this hasty, unseemly entrance, Your Holiness, but the guards are bringing the culprit here. He refused to answer us. Before you, he may speak.'

The Priest King nodded.

Two more guards entered, dragging along an unwilling, hostile kidnapper.

'Speak, prisoner,' ordered the Priest King.

He started asking questions. The prisoner replied reluctantly to them, though the questions were simple.

'Your name?'

'Anoush.'

'Your land?'

'Sutkagen Dor, on the river Dasht, in Makran.'

'Now tell us the reason for this horrific deed.'

There was a sullen silence for a while. Then in a complete turnaround the man started shouting, 'All this is his fault! I only wanted revenge because I had been imprisoned in Lothal for stealing two goats after knocking out a villager! But he . . . he wanted power and . . .'

He continued in this vein, but with so many foreign words it was difficult to understand what he was saying.

Finally a much-travelled merchant who could understand his language explained everything.

'Anoush and his companion had hatched this plan of revenge, and hoped to gain power by stealing the famed necklace.

'Actually, in the beginning it was only the necklace they wanted, but then they heard the monk's story and became greedy for the cloth too. They have been outlawed from their homeland, and thought that acquiring the necklace would give them untold power, and maybe one of them would one day become the Priest King in their land! They didn't even think about all the prayers, penance, self-denial and knowledge you have to acquire over the years for that.'

'They seriously thought that?' asked an incredulous and angry Priest King. 'I can't imagine anyone could be so stupid!'

The merchant talked rapidly to Anoush and then told the assembled crowd what he said.

'Sir, he is one of a tribe of marauders who trouble Meluhhan traders carrying our goods there. He came by boat to Lothal and met his friend, also from Sutkagen Dor . . . we will see him soon. The other guards have taken a boat to the island and they will soon be here with him.

'Coming back to this man, he was put in prison, sentenced by Your Excellency, though you may not remember him. But because he was a foreigner he was treated quite leniently. He had to fetch water, sweep the prison rooms and work in the fields. This made him so angry he decided he would take revenge on whoever had given this sentence. When he heard that the Priest King would be coming here, he went to the village where his friend was living and together they hatched this evil plan. The monk bringing the holy silk cloth was an even better opportunity for them. This prisoner thought that the people of Harappa would be disgraced, and the greatest dishonour would fall upon you, Sir.

'You would be removed from your position, then there would be chaos and anarchy, as there would be no one in power. He would meanwhile escape and quietly return to Sutkagen Dor Prahag, where he would become a chieftain and collect a band of followers, and start building an empire for himself, sending word to people as far away as Dakin that he knew the secret of making silk. Foolish man!

'He's the one who threw the stone to upset the ox near the river . . . so a distraction was created, and time was gained for them to kidnap Ketika and Keshav. He has even confessed to setting the storeroom on fire. Also, this fitted his idea of revenge very well . . . destroying stored grain.'

Avani exclaimed, 'Oh, now I know! I saw them talking on the day of the fire, but they looked different, wearing turbans and him with a flowing red beard; they were talking in one of the sheds, they sounded so angry I ran off to tell someone . . . but after the fire they vanished. But why set it on fire? What was the point?'

'Oh, they wanted to spite us, and what better way than destroying our grain? Then they thought we'd blame Sonu for it . . .

'Both Anoush and his friend constantly disguised themselves in different clothes and hairstyles, sometimes braided, sometimes tied, or a flowing beard, so people would think they were traders come from afar, and no one would recognize them. They eavesdropped on the children and got to know of Bhoot Byet. That's where Anoush hid. They got the children into trouble too, so that they were never allowed to go to Bhoot Byet, and would not discover Anoush's secret hiding-place.'

At this point a voice thundered, 'You, prisoner Anoush! Did you destroy grain for a petty motive like revenge and to see us suffer? And get an innocent man like hard-working Sonu deliberately blamed? That is unforgivable . . . two more unforgivable crimes! You deserve a harsh sentence.'

Everyone looked astounded. The voice belonged to the Priest King! He had been sitting in stern silence till then but now the wrath on his normally calm face was unmistakable.

'They were very evil to kidnap Ketika,' added the grim voice of Avani's baba. 'Unpardonable!'

Now all the mysteries had been solved except the most important one.

Who was the other kidnapper who had thought of this preposterous plan?

They were to know shortly.

Two guards entered, pulling a man along.

Everyone's mouths fell open in shock and amazement!

This man! They knew him so well! He was a trusted part of their community. He had helped them so often. They just could not believe it! This snarling face, with its malevolent look . . . could it be the same kind and helpful person they met everyday?

Hiroo! Hiroo da! Wearing a brown turban covering his face, his neatly tied brown beard left open . . .

Hiroo who had helped at the fire . . . Hiroo who had cleaned the temple altar . . .

This was a different face they were seeing. The mask had fallen off.

The air rang with enraged accusations.

'You deceitful person!'

'You betrayed our trust!'

'Evil man!'

'Harming our daughter!'

'Injuring our son-in-law!'

The shouts grew deafening.

The Priest King raised his hand high and there was instant silence.

'These scoundrels will be tried and punished for their duplicity, evil doings, treachery and betrayal of Harappan hospitality.'

Hiroo, a furious, but suddenly scared and badly scratched Hiroo, blustered and cringed on hearing this. 'It's a mistake! he shouted. 'I don't know anything, he did it all,' pointing to Anoush.

There was an acrimonious exchange between the two, each wanting to save his skin, incensed with the other. Confusion and noise prevailed. Finally the Priest King said in measured tones, 'Take them away.'

Rarely used harsh Harappan laws would finally be implemented! Justice would be delivered.

***

After a few days, Ketika and Keshav went off to Lothal, while the Priest King and the Chinese monks left for Mohenjo daro. There, Zhao Gao recognized the temple as the one he had seen in his visions, and his gratitude knew no bounds. After a purifying wash in the Great Bath, he prayed at the temple and invoked his ancestor gods. The Priest King then placed the cloth carefully in a secret alcove in the temple.

In Gola Dhoro and Bagasra, however, the excitement of the events that had taken place just didn't die down.

The four children continued their daily life but became the centre of admiration of the younger ones, and they had to repeat the story many times. The other children were fascinated by Manimaoo the cat, who they thought had been very clever. They tried to make friends with him, but he continued to ignore everyone except Avani. And for her, he was the biggest hero!

These happenings were the talk of the town for a long time. For many years, Avani and her friends would tell the exciting story of the kidnapping of the Priest King's daughter-in-law. Tavishi's and Avani's mothers were full of pride. Their brave girls! They had brought honour to the village of Bagasra.

What a day it had been! What a wedding it had been!

Tavishi and Avani were lauded for their courage,

loyalty and quick thinking, and were the heroines of the hour. Ambar and Delshad were also praised for rescuing Keshav.

The parents were proud of their Harappan girls!

A NOTE ON THE HARAPPAN
CIVILIZATION

In 1920–21, archaeologists discovered two large mounds that were possibly signs of an ancient civilization, These turned out to be the remains of the earliest civilization in India, much before the Aryans came in. The first mound unearthed a city called Harappa and the second, a city that was named Mohenjo daro. As Mohenjo daro was found on the banks of the Indus River, this civilization is known as either the Harappan or the Indus Valley Civilization. Archaeologists usually refer to it simply as the Harappan civilization, because of evidence which ties together all the settlements, towns, cities, hamlets and camps that existed during the same period, with similarities in food, clothing and shelter.

This civilization was spread over a vast geographic area, of 1.3 million square kilometres, larger than other ancient civilizations like Egypt and Mesopotamia. It extended over Pakistan, Punjab, Rajasthan, Gujarat, Uttar Pradesh, Jammu and even included Afghanistan and the Makaran coast of Baluchistan. The golden age of this civilization was from 2600 BCE to 1900 BCE, called the Mature Harappan age.

It was a very exciting discovery, as the archaeologists found all kinds of items, including jewellery, pottery, tools, terracotta figurines, vessels and various objects used in the daily life of people, who lived there more than 5,000 years ago.

Human bones were found, proving that people used to be buried in those times, and so were bones of animals, so we know which animals existed then.

A famous artefact that has been discovered is the small bronze figurine of a young dancing girl. So we know that they worked with metals and made beautiful and useful objects for which they must have needed great scientific knowledge. Stone and terracotta statues and toys were also made. The most famous of these is the stone bust of a bearded man, thought to be a priest or ruler . . . but no one knows for sure. They had no fuel, no electricity, no power of any kind and yet they made so many beautiful things!

We know that the Harappan people lived in cities as well as villages. Some cities may have had about 40,000 people living in them. The major cities were Harappa, Mohenjo daro, Lothal, Banawali, Meghrrgr, Kuntasi, Kalibangan and Dholavira. These people had the best town planning of ancient times, and even today people marvel at their advanced drainage and plumbing system, which kept the towns clean. There was clean drinking water for everyone. They used baked bricks to build their houses, which have lasted for thousands of years till today, and did not crumble due to the effect of water and sun. The bricks were all one size, as were their weights, which is proof of the attention they paid to detail. Grain was collected from agricultural villages and sent to be stored in granaries, which were built on raised platforms in Mohenjo daro and Harappa, so no one would starve in times of famine or floods.

A harp-like instrument was found, so we know they enjoyed music, and we can imagine them singing and dancing, and engaging in other social activities.

Cloth was made of wool and cotton. Necklaces, beads, amulets made of gold, silver, or semi-precious stones like carnelian and lapis lazuli have been discovered as well.

The Harappans also traded with other countries. Merchants took precious ivory, spices, timber, copper, carnelian and cotton from here, going by land through the Bolan Pass and crossing high mountains. They also went by sea to Mesopotamia, Iran and the Gulf countries. Seals have been found inscribed with pictures of boats and carts. These seals are tablets, made of soft steatite stone with intricate carvings. Unfortunately the script has not been deciphered, so no one knows exactly what each picture and each marking means. Perhaps they were used as labels for trading.

These people worshipped nature and trees. Their children played many games. Toys such as a toy cart, clay dolls, tops and even chess figurines have been found!

They seem to have been a peaceful people, as there is not much evidence of warfare.

But this civilization suddenly declined. Was there a flood, or a famine or invasion by warriors, or did they just not get enough food and water and people moved away? No one knows. However, they left behind evidence of a culture that had produced beautiful objects and of a prosperous land where there was peace.

Other Books in the Series

A CHOLA ADVENTURE

Anu Kumar

990 CE, Tanjore, India

Twelve-year-old Raji is growing up during the reign of Rajaraja Chola in the south of India. Raji is a girl of spirit-brave, bright and bold. She is also a dancer, a warrior and a sculptor who models kingdoms in stone. Raji, however, is not happy: She misses her family. Her mother is in exile and her father has left home in grief.

On a dark night as a storm rages, Raji rescues a Chinese sailor at sea. This sets off a chain of events with unforeseen consequences.

A Shiva statue goes missing, a prince disappears and there is a murder inside a temple. As Raji and her friends, the prince Rajendra Chola and his cousin, Ananta, try to help the Chinese mariner, they realize that he may have some of the answers Raji has been looking for.

Will the criminals be brought to justice? Will Raji's family be reunited once again? Will peace be restored to the mighty Chola Kingdom?

Other Books in the Series

A MAURYAN ADVENTURE

Subhadra Sen Gupta

3rd century BCE, Pataliputra, India

Madhura is twelve and lives in the legendary city of Pataliputra during the reign of King Ashoka of the Mauryan dynasty. She works in the palace as the maid and companion of Princess Sanghamitra.

Madhura does not like it all! Life is so boring. She dreams of travelling across the land like her brother Kartik, who is a trader and growing up to become a soldier, fighting with swords and riding horses.

Madhura's dreams suddenly come true as she travels with Kartik from Pataliputra to Ujjaini in a caravan. On the way mysterious things begin to happen. Who is that fat man who gives Kartik packets full of gold and silver coins? Why are they stopping at Vidisha to meet a Buddhist monk? Kartik is up to something and Madhura has to find out the truth.

Read this fascinating account of Madura's life, and discover what it was like to grow up in the past!